Thomas Nix

Thomas Nix

**A Serialized Novel by
Wesley Adams and Daphne McGee**

Book 4 of the Soap Opera Inspired Story Collection
Series Created by Gary Brin

Episodes 1-5

Painting of Paul LeMoyne by Jean-Auguste-Dominique Ingres
Cover photograph courtesy of Wikimedia Commons.
Cover photograph was digitally enhanced and visually altered for this edition.
Cover design and book layout © 2021 by Standish Press

FIRST EDITION

ISBN—978-1-945510-03-8

MANUFACTURED IN THE UNITED STATES OF AMERICA

To all great stories written throughout the course of world history—both published and unpublished—originality cannot be duplicated—at least not successfully anyway.

Hopefully books never become obsolete.

Contents

Intro

Thomas Nix was inspired in various ways by the classic novels *Vampyre* (1819) by John William Polidori, *Carmilla* (1872) by Joseph Sheridan Le Fanu, *Dracula* (1897) by Bram Stoker, and *Salem's Lot* (1975) by Stephen King. As well as the TV series *Dark Shadows* (1991 version) created by Dan Curtis and *Buffy the Vampire Slayer* (1996-2003 TV version) created by Joss Whedon. Special shout out also for the popular moody atmosphere monster-of-the-week TV series *Grimm* (2011-2017) created by David Greenwalt, Jim Kouf, and Stephen Carpenter based upon stories by the Brothers Grimm. And of course, last but not least, the 1979 above-average two-part miniseries based upon the previously-mentioned Stephen King novel, considered by many to be the best vampire movie adaption ever filmed. Thanks.

Thomas Nix was written in a serialized way in order to continue similarly formatted themes from classic prime-time soaps of the 1980s—but with present-day mature adult storylines added. It was written with the intention that it's playing to a visual audience and therefore will emulate a scripted format (without camera angle directions) rather than the usual storytelling methods displayed in popular full-length novels such as the 1975 novel *Salem's Lot* by Stephen King or the 1982 novel *Seventh Child* by Brooks Stanwood. It should also be noted that each episode of this series were written in a brief span of 6-12 days or less and therefore shouldn't be confused with being great literature. The goal of this series is to mimic episodes of popular modern-day soap operas or filmed YouTube web series dramas from enterprising filmmakers—by creating visual entertainment on a printed page—and not to create a literary masterpiece.

The storyline in *Thomas Nix* takes place about the same time the events in *Desperate Lives* occurred on an island in the Caribbean Sea. Characters from *Glass Owl* and *Desperate Lives* are featured in this novel as part of the present ongoing story.

Gary Brin
Series Creator

In an effort to have an accurate portrayal of the dialogue used for the *Soap Opera Inspired Story Collection Series* people were anonymously observed in shopping malls, schools, places of employment, and on public streets in order to capture a definitive portrayal of how people of various ages and cultures interacted and talked to each other when they thought no one was listening. While some select dialogue was exaggerated for dramatic purposes when needed—the manner and tone of which people were observed speaking to each other in casual and private conversations is accurate. Exact wording was not copied verbatim for the most part, but the way certain types of topics and conversations are addressed by characters in this serialized series is based on actual situations that were observed over a period of several dozen years.

Prologue

1
Castle Beach, Massachusetts
Late 1790

A young man walks back and forth after he gets out of a carriage. He stares at his father with a dazed look. Seconds later he collapses in a heap just inches away from the older man who seems confused by what is happening. The man looks up at his stern father with a pleading look and cries out in anguish.

"Father, I'm not well. Please call a doctor."

The older man looks at his son with harsh caution.

"Did you disobey me and venture into a tavern before you boarded your carriage in Boston for the trip back home?"

The young man shakes his head.

"No father, I gave you my word I wouldn't go."

The cold look of the older man makes it clear he doesn't believe what he's hearing. They look at each other for a few seconds as the young man begins to shake uncontrollably.

"Please father. Help me."

The carriage footman comes forward and shrugs.

"Should we call a doctor for Master Nix?"

The footman and the stern-looking older man glare at each other for a few seconds. Finally the older man nods and turns to look toward the cobblestone-lined street ahead.

"Doctor Sherwood lives two blocks away."

The footman nods and leaves. The young man seems to be staring up at the sky but seeing nothing as his father still retains the rigid look from earlier. He throws up his hands clearly upset at what he perceives is his son's betrayal. He sighs.

2

"I know not what is wrong with young Mr. Nix."

The doctor looks at the angry glare on the older man's face. He turns to look at the bedridden man before him and shakes his head. He watches the faces of the other people in the room as he quickly scrawls a few words on a piece of paper.

"This will help his pain."

He hands the piece of paper to the older man and sighs.

"I fear he will probably expire by nightfall."

One of the people in the room is an older woman. She slowly dabs her eyes with her handkerchief a few times.

"But what could have afflicted him so?"

Doctor Sherwood shakes his head again.

3

"Mother, please help me from this darkness."

The woman looks down at the man lying before her as her daughter wipes her brother's forehead with a cloth rag. He seems to become more delirious as his audience ignores his pleas.

"But I told you what I saw."

He tries to sit up in bed and winces.

"I saw eyes that glowed bright yellow."

He waves his hand frantically in the air like a ragdoll.

"Eyes and teeth I saw. Sharp teeth like a dog."

Both women turn to look at Doctor Sherwood nervously.

Page 14

"Could he be afflicted by a witch's spell like so happened last year with Mistress Robinson and two of her children?"

Eyes fall upon the doctor.

"Mistress Robinson and her children did not die because of witchcraft. They froze while attempting to cross Pall River."

The two women look at each other oddly.

"But Mistress Brewster said?"

Doctor Sherwood looks at the young man again and realizes he's dead. He reaches out to close the young man's eyes as the others in the room react. Loud wails can be heard.

4

A small group of people follow a coffin as it is carried through the doors of a mausoleum. Rain begins to fall lightly and then a little bit harder. Inside the mausoleum the coffin is carried inside a large room-like crypt and blessed repeatedly as several members of the mourning party repeat prayers. One of the mourners steps forth and places a crucifix on top of the coffin as it is laid into position in the middle of the room. A few minutes later after everyone says their goodbyes, the door to the crypt is put into place and sealed as a prayer is read aloud throughout. Nightfall is fast approaching as creeping shadows begin to dance joyfully about the inky blackness with deliberate swiftness.

A Brief Look at the First Episode

A peaceful New England village finds itself facing a nightmare as a mysterious stranger comes to town intent on exacting revenge for a punishment given to him several centuries previously.

Night Song

1
Castle Beach, Massachusetts
Present Day

"I thought I told you already I'm not ready."

David Sherwood slowly leans over to kiss his girlfriend and then attempts to unbutton her blouse. He seems annoyed.

"You can't stall anymore Susan. Time's up. I want to have sex with you in the backseat of my car. My rep is at stake."

David tries again to unbutton Susan's blouse.

"It's no big deal OK? You know my rep. I've been with a lot of girls. So what? Besides a guy without a rep is a total loser."

He laughs as he kisses Susan Lancaster again.

"We've been together one month already."

Susan seems uneasy.

"I just don't want to end up another one of many."

David gestures with his hand.

"Losing your virginity to me is expected—besides, better me than some stuck up rich geeky jerk from Pinecrest Prep."

Susan looks at David oddly.

"You know about Chandler Penney?"
David nods.
"Everyone knows. That loser is the talk of Castle Beach."
Susan sighs loudly.
"Chandler is a nice guy."
David rolls his eyes knowingly.
"Uh-huh—except for what he did."
Susan looks at David curiously.
"What are you talking about?"
David tries to kiss Susan once more.
"Old man Pendergraft."
"What about him?"
David leans over to whisper in Susan's ear. She seems shocked at what she's hearing. They look at each other.
"He wouldn't."
"He did."
David leans back on the park bench.
"Plowed into him like garbage—didn't stop either."
Susan takes a deep breath.
"How come I never heard that story?"
David waves his hand.
"Chandler's dad paid off Orville Pendergraft."
Susan takes another deep breath.
"How do you know?"
David grins broadly and winks.
"Working part time at the DMV has its perks."
He laughs slyly.
"Still think Chandler Penney is a nice guy?"
Susan turns away from David.
"He just drove away?"
"Uh-huh."
David pulls Susan toward him.
"I really like you."
He kisses her lightly on the lips again and smirks.
"Let's just have sex already. I'm really horny."
He slides his fingers across her breasts and grins slyly.

"I promise I'll be gentle."

He kisses her again. Susan aggressively pushes him away and gives him a harsh stare as David sighs loudly in protest.

2

Two teenage boys slowly walk toward a thick overgrowth of thorny shrubs partially hidden among a tangle of vines and dead trees. They seem to be looking for something and stop every few minutes. Overhead clouds seem to be forming.

3

"Oh my God he's slick."

Kyle Webster grins as he turns to look at his best friend Preston Sago. He makes a lewd gesture with his finger.

"He's gonna get Susan soon from the way he's playing her. She'll be just another number when they finish fucking in the backseat of his car. I wish I could score as easily as he does."

Preston jabs Kyle.

"Ever wonder why you strike out so often?"

Kyle turns to face Preston.

"*No*—but do tell."

Preston glances at David and Susan kissing and turn to look at Kyle. He adjusts the mirror inside his car and laughs.

"Girls don't date guys that dress dorky."

Kyle shrugs.

"I don't dress dorky."

Preston laughs.

"Keep telling yourself that."

Kyle looks at David and Susan again.

"I've had girlfriends."

Preston rolls his eyes and laughs.

"Uh-huh—for like a day or two. Then they score with one of the jocks and you're left out in the cold—rejected."

Kyle nervously glances at himself in the rearview mirror.

Page **19**

"I've been told I have a pleasant personality."

Preston rolls his eyes and smirks.

4

A car pulls up outside a small building and seconds later a man steps out. He heads toward the front door. Above the front door a plain-printed sign reads in bold letters DAILY SPILL.

5

"Why don't you sign up?"

"You really think I have a chance?"

Jessica Sago turns around to look at her teacher Milton Donovan. He pulls out a pen and gives it to her. She sighs.

"But what if I'm no good?"

Milton glances at the bulletin board in front of him.

"You won't know unless you try."

Jessica looks at the pen in her hand and then at Milton.

"I've never published anything before."

Milton looks at Jessica curiously and smiles.

"But you've written plenty."

He glances at the bulletin board again.

"Your essays are the best in my class. Better than most I've seen in ten years. Take a chance already. Dare to try."

They look at each other for a few a seconds.

6

Megan Bowers fumbles with the keys to her car as she looks back at the house in front of her. She seems upset.

"Cheating bastard—wish I had a gun."

She unlocks the door and as she's about to get into the car a man comes running out of the house clad only in black boxer briefs. Malcolm Kingsbury stops suddenly and yells loudly.

"She means nothing to me."

Megan looks at Malcolm for a few seconds and then slams the door to her car shut. Tears stream down her cheeks.

"It's over."

Malcolm watches as she starts the engine to the car.

"Can't we discuss this? I love you."

Megan rolls her eyes.

"You have a funny way of showing it."

Malcolm looks down at his stiff erection straining against the confines of his underwear. He grins slyly and laughs.

"It just happened. One thing led to another."

Megan notices a movement at the front door.

"I'll just bet."

Malcolm turns around to see Lisa Morgan standing in the doorway with her hands on her hips. She's wearing a robe.

"Forget about her already."

She watches as Megan drives away.

"She's a frigid bitch—always has been—even back in high school. You're better off without her. I'm what you need."

She glances at his erection.

"How about we pick up where we left off earlier before we were so rudely interrupted by my half-sister and her lecture."

Malcolm glances at Megan's car as it turns the corner and disappears from view. He faces Lisa. She pulls open her robe.

"Do what you do best."

He grins broadly and follows her into the house.

7

As the front door opens Greg Petrie looks up to see Maxwell Pendergraft closing the door behind him. He grins.

"Never thought I'd see you here again?"

Maxwell smirks and waves his hand.

"Your words not mine."

He walks toward where Greg is sitting at his desk.

"Pop had to be moved from Clearview."

Greg shakes his head.

"Sorry about your dad. Still can't believe that spoiled brat got off easy. But then again *his* kind always skirts the law."

Maxwell sits at the edge of the desk.

"Not this time."

Greg looks at Maxwell curiously.

"Got a plan in motion?"

Maxwell shrugs.

"Just got a new lawyer out of Boston last week—he seems to think we can still bring charges against the Penney family."

Greg rolls his eyes.

"So many have tried to bring them down?"

Maxwell pulls out a piece of paper from the back pocket of his Levi's and hands it to Greg. They look at each other.

"Seems young Mr. Penney has been flirting with the law in all sorts of sneaky ways. Unfortunately for him I found out."

He laughs.

"I intend to work that angle."

Greg leans back in his chair and laughs.

"I want first dibs on the story."

Maxwell grins.

"I'll think about it."

Greg sits up.

"Hey?"

Maxwell laughs.

"Of course the story is yours. Relax already."

He leans across the desk.

"I'm taking Pop to Whispering Hills in about an hour or so if they work fast enough—waiting for the paperwork to clear."

"That place is pricey."

Maxwell stands up and grins broadly.

"Uh-huh—but Penney is paying for it. Choked every dollar I could get out of Carson Penney and his terrible brood."

He sighs loudly.

"Pop deserved better than he got."

Greg nods in agreement.

8
Boston

Carson Penney looks at the folder in his hand and then back at Jeremy Winterfield. He seems in shock and sighs.

"This is an outrage."

Jeremy leans back in his chair and grins.

"Nevertheless your son is going to face what he did."

Carson tosses the folder on top of the desk.

"I'll destroy you."

Jeremy rolls his eyes.

"Who do you think you're playing with here—some rookie amateur dealing with his first case? Your son is going to pay for what he did. There's no way out. The time when you and others like you could pay off people to look the other way is over."

Jeremy leans forward.

"I've never lost a case. Not ever."

He laughs.

"Know why Penney?"

He grins slyly.

"I play dirty. No reason to pretend. If you fuck with me I fuck back one hundred times harder. I don't stop until I win. And I'll do anything I have to in order to win—plain and simple."

Carson clenches his fists.

"I'll crush you."

Jeremy stands up.

"Bad move to threaten me Penney."

He walks over to where Carson is standing.

"Like I said I play dirty."

He leans over and whispers in Carson's ear.

"If you so much as try to play one of your games and send your goons after me or anyone I know—I'll fight back hard."

He laughs loudly.

"Think before you act Penney. It'll be a really bad scene if some accident befalls your children. I mean, let's face it—your precious daughter could have all sorts of things happening around her or *to* her. Would be a shame if she was abducted or worse if she was raped on some lonely stretch of road just outside of that quaint little town you call home. And your youngest boy, oh, such a terrible thing without a doubt if he were kidnapped and held for ransom by someone who had a penchant for young boys, and oh, it would be so sad indeed if your family had to deal with such tragedy on top of your eldest facing charges for what he did weeks ago. Yep, I'd really think about what I just said."

Carson seems aghast.

"You'll never get away with it."

Jeremy snaps his fingers gleefully.

"How about we test that theory shall we?"

Jeremy looks back at his desk.

"From here on out you and your family are on borrowed time. I've got lots of connections, more than you do. And I'm not afraid to play them. Your family means nothing to me. Their lives are worthless as far as I'm concerned. If you cross me I'll make sure you pay dearly. Not one member of your loved ones will get out of this mess unscathed—not even your dead wife."

Carson seems confused. Jeremy grins slyly.

"Crypts are vandalized every day. Coffins are opened. Stuff happens—something else for you to think about in addition to what I said about your precious family. I'll do whatever I have to do to beat you. Be prepared. I don't make idle threats."

They look at each other.

"Oh, I almost forgot. That little business deal with the Russians you think no one knows about—won't be secret much longer. It would be a shame if the government found out."

Jeremy picks up the folder from on top of the desk.

"Take this home with you and think about it."

He shoves it in Carson's hand.

"And for the record I wouldn't try to play anyone against me because I'll find out rather quickly. And once I do, the first part of my plan goes into motion. Have a nice day Penney."

Carson seems in shock as he walks to the door. He turns around once to look at Jeremy angrily. Jeremy grins broadly.

9

Susan pushes David away as he begins to unbutton her blouse. He seems confused by her cold behavior and sighs.

"This is as good a day as any."

"I need more time to think about it."

David seems inpatient.

"I'm the only guy for you."

He laughs.

"Everyone you know will applaud you once they find out you finally gave it up to me. Seriously, you're one of the few sad sack holdouts left that think we're still living back in 1955."

Susan pushes David away.

"You knew the kind of girl I was before we started hanging out together. I wasn't like Natalie or Isabel. I'm better."

David seems upset.

"Is this your way of telling me you're never going to give it up to me? I think I have a right to know if that's the case."

Susan buttons her blouse once more.

"I never said I wouldn't."

David leers at Susan. She sighs loudly.

"But I never said I would either."

David seems upset as Susan turns away.

10

Greg and Maxwell shake hands briefly as Greg looks up at the DAILY SPILL sign. He and Maxwell look at each other.

"When my dad retired last year he made me promise I wouldn't run his newspaper into the ground. Sometimes I think he loved the paper more than he did me or my mother."

"It's quite a tough act to follow if I do say so myself."

Greg shrugs knowingly.

"Tell me about it."

They shake hands again.

"It's just another hundred feet or so."

Chris Gibson turns around to look at his cousin as they reach a clearing amid a tangle of shrubs and prickly vines.

"I saw it when we went ballooning last fall. There's a graveyard somewhere in these woods—plenty of headstones."

Parker Ross peers into the expanse of thick vines.

"Place probably has lots of booby traps."

Chris laughs loudly.

"It's a cemetery—not a frigging bunker Parker."

"No one has been out here in years."

Chris rolls his eyes.

"Duh—that's why it's so exciting."

He takes a step forward.

"Think of what we could find."

Parker sighs loudly.

"Uh-huh—that's what I'm afraid of. Skeletons aren't my thing, OK. Dead people, ugh. Hate cemeteries with a passion."

Chris grabs Parker.

"I didn't come this far to turn back now."

He forcibly pushes Parker through the shrubbery.

"Who knows we might find lost treasure or something?"

Parker stops and looks at Chris.

"Lost treasure in a cemetery? I think not."

They come to another clearing.

"I heard some old folks in town talking about it."

Chris stops and looks around.

"They said there was a sailor who visited Castle Beach back in the 1800s and he buried some of his loot in the woods by the cemetery—said he hid a map inside the mausoleum at the entrance to the boneyard—then went back to sea and never came back. No one ever found his loot—at least not yet."

Parker looks at Chris suspiciously.

"I'm not breaking into a mausoleum."

Chris aggressively jabs Parker.

"Oh yeah you are."

Parker looks at the thick woods ahead.

"No way—I draw the line at breaking into some broken down burial vault. There's probably bones scattered inside."

Chris laughs.

"Don't be a puss OK—there are no bones just lying around on the floor. They're all inside vaults—out of sight and mind."

Parker sighs loudly.

"Let's just go back—let's forget this whole breaking into a creepy old mausoleum deal to find some stupid map left behind by some long-dead sailor from way back in ancient times."

Chris grabs Parker and shoves him.

"We're not turning back."

He clenches his hand into a fist.

"I'll bust you if I have to."

Parker looks at the angry scowl on his cousin's face.

"I hate you."

Chris laughs.

"Tell it to someone who cares."

He laughs loudly and pushes Parker.

12

Boston

Carson leans against his car and sighs loudly as he looks at the folder in his hand. He seems worried and sighs again.

"What the hell am I going to do?"

He looks at his watch.

"Winterfield knows he wouldn't get away with what he threatened to do if I call his bluff. He knows I'm a force to be reckoned with in New England. Knows I can cause serious havoc in his life if he dares to come up against me. But what if he makes good on his threat? Things could really get out of hand."

He pulls out his cell phone.

Page **27**

13

Megan wipes a tear from her eye as she slowly pulls into a parking lot. She begins to cry—then stops suddenly and blinks.

"I won't let him turn my life into a reality show."

She wipes away more tears.

"He and Lisa deserve each other."

She sighs.

"Lisa has always been a slut—gave it up for every boy in high school that pretended to like her—but Malcolm—he?"

She turns to look at herself in the rearview mirror and wipes away a few more tears. She rubs her cheeks briefly.

"He said he loved me."

She glances at her cell phone.

"I'll make them both pay for what they did to me."

She smiles slyly.

"Uh-huh—and I know just the person to ask."

She picks up her cell phone.

14

"I still think this is a mistake."

Shirley Brewster looks at the computer screen again.

"Isn't there another way?"

On the computer screen through a live link Matt Brewster shakes his head. He holds up a sheet of paper in his hand.

"There's no way out of it Shirley. Numbers don't lie. This is your cousin speaking—it's time to pull the plug—do it."

"But I worked so hard."

Matt shakes his head several times.

"I'm sorry but you asked me for my opinion."

Shirley sighs loudly.

"OK—OK—it's just so hard."

They look at each other.

"How do I tell Clyde?"

Matt grimaces.

Page **28**

"Better sooner than later."
He holds up additional paperwork.
"Clyde will understand."
Shirley shakes her head and turns away.
"He trusted me."
She looks at a picture of an older man holding up a string of fish looking out at the open ocean behind him. She sighs.
"Take the offer from McKay Enterprises."
Matt holds up another piece of paper to the screen as Shirley nods. He waves his hand in the air and smiles.
"Clyde Walker might surprise you."
Shirley nods again.

15

"Yes. That's right."
Megan sighs loudly as she wipes away another tear.
"I want you to wipe out his bank account."
She rolls her eyes.
"Of course I know it's my money. Malcolm has never worked a day in his life. Everything he has belongs to me."
She smiles broadly.
"Tomorrow is perfect. He'll hate it."
She laughs.
"Uh-huh—leave a smiley face when you're done."
She wipes away another tear.
"I know. I know."
She nods a few times.
"Without a doubt I want that cheating boyfriend of mine to know I'm behind this deal. Ugh, check that—ex-boyfriend."
She looks at the cell phone.
"Oh yeah, I almost forgot—last year he had a party at his apartment and got so zonked he kissed the pizza delivery guy."
Megan smirks.
"French kissed him actually."
She licks her lips.

Page **29**

"I'll send you the video. Load it up to YouTube with the caption "Malcolm Kingsbury and His Boyfriend" and include a few comments just for good measure. That'll teach Lisa a lesson."

She licks her lips again.

"Appreciate it."

She shuts off her cell phone and grins.

"He's not sorry yet but he will be."

She looks around.

"They both will be when I'm finished with them."

She steps out of her car.

16

Chris and Parker come toward another clearing and stop suddenly. A few yards away amid the tangle of dead trees and vines they look in awe as a cemetery comes into view. Chris takes a step forward as Parker grabs his arm and sighs loudly.

"Let's go back."

Chris rolls his eyes.

"Like hell."

He grins broadly as he jerks free of Parker's grip.

"There's loot buried around here somewhere and I'm going to find it. I'll be so rich I'll be able to buy that mansion out by Rocky Point—heard it was priced at four million smackers."

Parker seems uneasy as he looks around.

"I have a bad feeling about this. Like really bad."

Chris ignores Parker and takes another step.

"You're a fucking embarrassment to our entire family. I swear you must be adopted. Total wimp you are. Ugh."

He stops and turns around to face his cousin. He raises his fist again. Parker looks at him curiously for a few seconds.

"I'm through being nice."

Chris shakes his fist.

"Keep up your whining and I'll be forced to work out my frustrations on your face—make you even less attractive than you already are. You make the call cousin—but beware my fist."

Page 30

Parker looks at Chris with a cold stare and then reluctantly follows his cousin through the broken gate of the cemetery.

17

"You're just lucky I'm a nice guy."

David runs his fingers through his hair as Susan ignores his comment. He seems upset as they walk toward a parking lot.

"Chandler Penney I'm not."

Susan stops and faces David.

"I still can't believe he did what you said."

David shrugs.

"Got no reason to talk trash about dear Chandler—he's a creep—thinks he can do whatever he wants when he chooses."

David grabs Susan's arm.

"He's also no charmer with the ladies either."

He sighs loudly.

"I have it on a good source he drugged Lily Blackwell at his house last year—and then he took her to his bedroom."

Susan seems shocked.

"She said nothing happened."

David rolls his eyes.

"That's what he told her. But he told his friends he scored big time. Bragged about how easy it was—said she was totally out of it as he did his thing—lied to her when she woke up."

David looks toward the highway nearby.

"But if you don't believe me why don't you take a chance with Chandler? See how long it'll take for him to play you?"

David makes a lewd gesture with his finger.

18
Boston

"What do you mean you'll pass on my offer?"

Carson angrily slams his fist down on a coffee table.

"I'll pay you triple."

Cole Franklin leans back on the sofa.

"Doesn't matter—not interested in any deal when it comes to Jeremy Winterfield. That dude is not to be messed with—all sorts of stories floating about town concerning his methods of dealing with anyone stupid enough to cross him for whatever reasons. Besides, I just got back from the United States Virgin Islands dealing with a job that didn't pay off. I need a few weeks to collect myself. But thanks again for thinking of me."

Carson glances at Cole curiously.

"Exactly what does Winterfield have on you?"

Cole sits up.

"Do yourself a favor and tell your son he's going to spend some time in the pen. Better him than you if truth be known."

Carson clenches his fists.

"How about I pay ten times your usual deal?"

Cole laughs.

"Not interested for any amount."

He sighs loudly.

"Show yourself out."

Carson looks at Cole oddly and leaves. As the door slams shut Cole shrugs and looks at the cell phone on top of his desk.

"Some people never learn."

He picks up his cell phone and begins dialing.

"Uh-huh—just like you said—but I told him I couldn't take him up on his offer. He was really pissed—threatened me."

Cole nods a few times and grins slyly.

"Thank you."

He slowly shuts off the cell phone and smiles broadly.

"So glad I'm not Penney."

He begins to laugh.

19

Chris takes a step toward the mausoleum entrance as Parker hangs back a few feet. The metal door is badly rusted, as is the lock hanging ominously on its hinges. Chris grins broadly.

"Looks just like the tacky Penney mausoleum at Rolling Meadows Memorial. Give or take the nice manicured lawns."

He looks up at the faded name NIX carved in bold lettering right above the entrance of the water-stained stone building.

"Nix—there's no one in town with that name?"

Chris seems confused and faces Parker.

"I think the last Nix died in Boston back in the 1980s."

Parker watches as Chris takes a step forward.

"Doesn't matter anyways—don't need permission from a bunch of dried-up bones. This lock poses no challenge to me."

He reaches out to grab the rusted lock and as he touches the top—it falls away. He looks back at Parker and laughs.

"Oops—lock—what lock?"

He pushes the door inward. A loud creaking sound is heard as the metal hinges squeak loudly. Chris peers inside the abandoned vault and grins broadly. Inside the single room, vaults line the walls. Years of neglect have stained the white marble with black-colored grime throughout. Off to one corner Chris notices a single crypt. On the door in faded gold-colored letters, the name THOMAS NIX is spelled out. Chris slowly enters as cobwebs stick to his clothing. He brushes them away and slowly walks across the marble floor. His footsteps echo loudly as he slowly approaches the door with the faded name printed on it.

"Give me your pocket flashlight Parker."

Chris turns around and realizes he's alone. Parker is nowhere to be found. He calls out but there's no answer.

"Goddamn prick."

He looks at his watch.

"I can't believe he bailed on me."

He wipes sweat from his brow and shrugs.

"Fuck him."

He looks around nervously.

"Still got time left to look around."

He notices the huge crucifix on the door for the first time amid the stains from years of neglect. He seems confused.

"Was this dude a religious nut?"

He glances at the other crypts lining the walls nearby and then faces the door again. He reads the dates under the name.

"BORN 1768—FOUND PEACE 1790."

He looks at the crucifix again and shrugs.

"Found peace? What the hell is that supposed to mean? Why couldn't they just say he died? Twenty-two years old. Oh man, wouldn't that be the worse deal—to die so young."

He examines the door to the large crypt more closely.

"I bet the map is hidden somewhere in there."

He looks at his watch once more.

"But where the fuck is the doorknob?"

He turns to look at the door again.

"There must be some sort of a trick panel to open it."

He notices the afternoon sun beginning to fade.

20

"What's going on Shirley?"

Clyde Walker looks at Shirley curiously as she tries to smile but does a bad job at it. She reaches out to pat his hand.

"I have some bad news."

She glances at the folder in her hand.

"I should've listened to you."

Clyde looks at the folder in Shirley's hand and seems to realize the truth. He takes a deep breath and rubs his eyes.

"I hope this isn't what I think it is?"

Shirley seems to be seconds away from crying.

21

"Hey, watch where you're going."

Parker looks up to see someone giving him their middle finger as they zip by. He recognizes Chandler Penney and flips him a finger in return. As he walks toward Castle Beach he turns every few seconds to look back to see if Chris is following him but there's no one there. He sighs loudly and continues walking.

22
Boston

"Uh-huh—that's right, the cemetery is just a ways up from the highway. You'll see the sign leading to Rolling Meadows Memorial with a huge arrow pointing toward the entrance right afterwards. Wait until the caretaker and his crew leave for the night. Jump the wall at the entrance and smash every one of the stained glass windows in the Penney mausoleum and then spray paint the name I gave you on the outside. Penney will get the message soon enough that I'm not to be trifled with. Bet you anything that piece of trash buckles to my will. His son is going to take a fall one way or the other—better sooner than later."

Jeremy laughs.

"What? Are you actually asking me such questions?"

He puts his feet on top of his desk and grins.

"Don't care about such things."

He rolls his eyes.

"Penney will bow to my will or else."

He begins laughing loudly.

23

Susan blinks several times as she glances at a huge movie poster just outside a small multi-screen movie theater.

"Susan?"

She turns around to see Claire Cassell looking at her with a mixture of pity and obvious amusement. She smiles weakly.

"I really don't want to go to work."

Claire begins to laugh.

"I don't blame you one bit. I hate this job as much as you do but at the moment we're both stuck working here."

They walk toward the entrance.

"Think Marlisa will be in a good mood today?"

Claire shrugs and seems annoyed.

"Doubtful."

They both glance knowingly at each other.

"If there was an award for being a lousy manager—she'd win hands down. I swear she seems to excel at being a bitch."

Susan nods and sighs loudly.

"Don't say that in public."

Claire makes a lewd gesture with her finger.

24

"Who the fuck designed this thing?"

Chris sighs as he searches the smooth marble door for an opening. He stops every few seconds to look at his hands and reacts to the grime that seems to get thicker each time he touches the faded marble surface. He shrugs and begins to slide his fingers over the visible cracks along the edge of the door.

"Damn it—why the fuck is there no opening?"

He takes a deep breath.

"Fuck."

He continues to slide his fingers along the crack and a few seconds later he hears a noise and realizes the heavy marble door is slightly ajar. He grins broadly and tries to peer inside.

"Pitch black."

He glances at the window.

"Poor guy—he's been laying in total darkness for over two hundred years—probably never got laid while he was alive."

He begins to laugh as he shakes his head.

"What the fuck am I doing feeling sorry for some dead guy from a rich family? Probably was a selfish toady bastard."

He forces the door to open further. As he does this, the huge stone crucifix on the door of the crypt falls to the floor and shatters into tiny pieces. Chris turns around and looks at the scattered pieces. He shrugs and turns toward the open door.

"This has to be where that old sailor hid his treasure map before he left town—and left all that loot for me to find."

He pushes the door further and peers into the crypt.

Page **36**

25

Parker stops in front of a movie theater and sees Susan and Claire behind the concession stand unpacking candy.

"Maybe I can score a free movie?"

He walks toward the entrance and stops. Out in the lobby he sees Marlisa Turner berating one of her employees.

"Doesn't she ever take a day off from work?"

He turns and begins walking down the street as he passes several teenagers who point at him and begin laughing.

26

"I'm so sorry."

Clyde looks at Shirley in shock.

"How could something like this happen?"

Shirley shakes her head.

"Business just totally dried up last December right before Christmas and I couldn't get it back on track. I'm so sorry."

Clyde looks at the paperwork in front of him.

27

Chandler seems irritated as he looks at his girlfriend Ivy Patterson. He reaches out to touch her again. She slaps him.

"I thought I just said I'm not in the mood."

Chandler grabs Ivy and pulls her toward him. He grins broadly as he kisses her. She pulls away and slaps him again.

"You disgust me."

Chandler gives Ivy an odd look.

"You're my girlfriend—act like it already."

Ivy wipes a tear from her eye.

"What about you and Susan Lancaster?"

Chandler reacts to the comment with a sneer.

"What about her?"

"You tried to score a date with her."

Chandler laughs.

"I did no such thing."

Ivy pulls out her cell phone.

"Heather Stamos says differently."

Chandler slowly runs his fingers through his hair.

"Heather is a lying busybody."

Ivy presses a few buttons on her cell phone.

"Is she really?"

Instantly a video plays across the screen of her cell phone as Chandler watches in shock knowing he's busted. He grins.

"So what—that proves nothing."

Ivy shuts off her cell phone.

"You said you'd never cheat on me again after what happened last month between you and Natalie Cassell. You said I was all you needed—said we had something really special."

Chandler rolls his eyes.

"We do—that video is bogus. Someone paid a model to pretend to be me. I was framed, OK—that guy isn't me."

Ivy looks at Chandler curiously.

"Do you actually think I'm that stupid?"

Chandler clenches his fist.

"How dare you accuse me of lying?"

Chandler seems to become enraged and grabs Ivy again as he forces himself on top of her. He pushes her down in the backseat of his car and rips her skirt as he tries to yank off her underwear. She screams loudly as he hits her again and again.

"From now on I call the shots."

He slaps her hard across her face. She continues to scream as he aggressively penetrates her. Her loud screams are drowned out by his laughter as he plows into her repeatedly, slapping her over and over until she finally becomes silent. Minutes later he pulls out and looks at Ivy with a look of joy and pity. He sighs.

"I call the shots until I say differently."

Ivy begins to cry. Chandler seems irritated.

"Shut up you stupid bitch."

He raises his hand and gives her a sharp look.
"Not another word out of you."
Ivy glances at her torn skirt as Chandler seems bored.
"Don't push me Ivy."
He flexes his muscular arms.

28

Malcolm looks over at Lisa lying next to him on the bed as the laughter from his cell phone echoes. He seems confused.
"Why would you think I'm gay?"
He looks at the cell phone confused.
"I never kissed a guy."
He reaches out to grab his laptop lying on a table next to the bed. He flips it open and seconds later he becomes enraged as he looks at footage of himself kissing a pizza delivery man. He clenches his fists as the laughter on the other end of the line appears to get louder. He watches Lisa's reaction and then shuts off the cell phone. He throws the laptop against the wall in a rage and seems about to explode over Megan's revenge.
"Goddamn Megan."
He looks at the shattered laptop lying on the floor.
"She's going to pay for this."
He turns to look at Lisa.
"Do you have any idea where that bitch sister of yours could be at this moment? I'm going to break her fucking neck."
Lisa shakes her head.
"Did you really kiss the pizza delivery guy?"
Malcolm turns to look at Lisa.
"Fuck you *bitch*."
Without warning he angrily grabs her by the neck.
"I don't do guys."
He twists her neck backwards.
"Goddamn stupid whore."
He jumps up and stomps out of the room.

Chris silently walks into the windowless room and as his eyes adjust to the pitch blackness he sees a coffin in the center on a raised step-like structure. He slowly approaches the coffin and notices a crucifix lying on top. He glances at the interior and seems impressed by the sheer expanse of the massive crypt.

"Thomas Nix must have been a really rich guy."

He walks closer to the coffin and casually reaches out to remove the crucifix. Chris looks at the dust-covered crucifix briefly and then lays it down on a ledge nearby. He looks at the coffin again and grins broadly as he runs his fingers along the top of the lid. He reaches out and pulls lightly. He sighs.

"I might as well see what the stiff looks like now."

His voice echoes throughout the crypt.

"This Nix dude is probably just a pile of dried-up bones. Like it's been two hundred plus years since he took a dirt nap."

He begins to whistle as he pulls the lid open. Chris seems annoyed as it appears unwilling to budge, squeaking loudly.

"Damn it—sounds like a horror movie."

He slowly pulls on the lid once again and finally it lifts.

"This is quite a moment without a doubt."

Chris looks in shock as the body in the coffin comes into view. He gasps as he stares at the perfectly-preserved body.

"What the fuck."

Chris continues staring at the corpse totally fascinated by what he's seeing. He pulls his eyes away for a few seconds.

"Wait till I tell Parker about this place."

He slowly turns to look around at the interior of the large crypt and sighs, then faces the open coffin once more and is shocked at what he sees before him. The coffin is empty.

"Where's the stiff?"

Chris hears a noise behind him and as he spins around he's grabbed by the neck. He reacts to seeing Thomas Nix staring at him with glowing eyes. His eyes are a bright hue of yellow surrounded by a dark red rim. Chris seems unable to move.

"You can't be real."
Chris tries to push Thomas away.
"Like what the fuck are you?"
Chris struggles to free himself as Thomas pulls him closer.
"You can't be."
Thomas grins broadly as Chris screams.
"Let go of me this instant."
Seconds later it's all over for Chris as Thomas hungrily satisfies his thirst. As he drinks, he begins to hum a tune of a long ago forgotten song while shadows of the night spring to life outside seeming to welcome the rebirth of their dark leader.

30

Dark gloom hangs everywhere as a lone black-clad figure silently walks through the woods. He stops and looks out at a small picturesque town in the distance. His eyes glow as his rage seems to overwhelm him while his quest for revenge grows.

TO BE CONTINUED

A Brief Look at the Second Episode

A mysterious stranger makes his way to town as the past and present come together while the personal lives of several townspeople start to fall apart caused by errors in judgment.

Episode 2
Castle Beach

1

Ivy Patterson wipes away semen from between her legs as Chandler Penney looks at her with a sly smirk. He laughs.

"How about you and me repeat what just happened tomorrow night? We've been sliding for months—but now."

Ivy tosses the soiled paper towel into her purse.

"I'm going to tell Chief Wheeling what you did to me."

Chandler seems about to explode.

"You'll do no such thing."

He aggressively grabs her.

"I'll ruin you."

Ivy pulls away from Chandler.

"You raped me."

Chandler bursts out laughing as he glances at his erection swelling under his corduroy jeans. He pulls Ivy toward him.

"I did no such thing."

He licks his lips several times and laughs.

"We did what couples usually do—we fucked. You're a whore and I'm a cool guy—popular with all your friends."

He angrily twists Ivy's arm backwards and watches her reaction. She tries to pull away. He seems to be enjoying the power he has over her at the moment. She cries out in pain.

"Let go of me this instant."

Chandler grins broadly as he applies even more force while he wrings her arm to one side. He leans toward her.

"If you say one word about any of this to anyone I assure you I'll make you regret it. I can do whatever I want in this town in case you still haven't figured it out. My family calls the shots."

He lets go of Ivy's arm.

"You raped me."

Chandler grabs Ivy again as his rage grows.

"I'm not going to warn you again."

He begins hitting her repeatedly as her screams echo loudly for a few seconds before silence permeates the area.

2

Parker Ross pushes the door inward to a small diner as the owner, Wendy Emerson, looks up from the gossip magazine she seems engrossed in. She smiles broadly as she sees him.

"I haven't seen you in a while?"

Parker closes the door behind him.

"I've been busy."

Wendy looks at Parker curiously and winks.

"Got a girlfriend?"

Parker shakes his head.

"I wish."

He walks over to the counter.

"Hey—I know you're quite the history buff for Castle Beach. At least I assume you are from what everyone says."

Wendy rolls her eyes knowingly.

"History buff not town gossip. There is a difference in case you confused the two together. I hope you see my point."

Parker smirks slyly as he looks at Wendy.

"Can you tell me anything about the Nix family?"

Wendy seems shocked at hearing the name mentioned. Parker notices. They share an uneasy moment of silence.

"Why do you ask?"

Parker turns to look at the empty diner.

"I'd rather not say just yet."

Wendy shrugs.

"Oh-oh—what has Chris done now?"

Parker turns away.

3

Malcolm Kingsbury pulls on a pair of jeans as Lisa Morgan looks at him confused. He faces her with a grin. As he reaches out to touch her with a smirk she pulls away. She seems upset.

"Don't touch me."

Malcolm looks at Lisa and rolls his eyes.

"You shouldn't have talked to me like that."

He winks at her.

"I lose control easily."

He pulls on his sneakers.

"It's a guy thing."

He stands up and walks to the door.

"When I get back we'll play."

Lisa rubs her neck for a few seconds.

"Don't bother."

Malcolm becomes enraged again and walks over to where Lisa is sitting on the bed. He angrily grabs her by the neck.

"I said I was sorry—case closed."

Lisa tries to pull away from Malcolm's grip.

"We're through."

Malcolm lets go of Lisa.

"Like hell we are. You broke up my relationship with your fucked-up half-sister. I'll decide when we're through. Not you."

He looks at himself in the mirror.

"Like I said we'll play when I get back."

He opens the bedroom door.

Page **45**

"But first I have to find that goddamned bitch and teach her a lesson for daring to fuck with me. I might just kill her."

He whistles loudly as he leaves the room.

4

"I'm so sorry I ruined your company."

Clyde Walker glances at Shirley Brewster as he shakes his head and looks at the signed papers. He faces her again.

"You didn't ruin my company Shirley. The economy ruined my business. These are tough times for anyone but especially from small outfits like mine. Businesses everywhere all over the country are folding or being bought up by other companies. At least you had the good sense to make a sweet deal with McKay Enterprises. Better a deal than no deal at all is what I say."

"I just feel so bad."

Clyde reaches out to pat Shirley's hand.

"I had to retire anyway. I'm not exactly forty."

He laughs.

"McKay Enterprises said they'd keep Walker Press running as a subsidiary—said the name wouldn't change. I guess I should be especially thankful for that—all my hard work will endure."

He smiles broadly.

"How about we grab a bite to eat at Emerson's Diner?"

He winks.

"Wendy Emerson has a sweet spot for me."

Clyde picks up the folder.

"I also want to talk to you about your cut of the deal. It's only fair—wouldn't be right otherwise Shirley—fair is fair."

Shirley seems confused.

"Cut of the deal?"

Clyde nods.

"Uh-huh."

Shirley seems uneasy.

"But it was my fault you lost Walker Press?"

Clyde waves his hand in the air.

Page **46**

"You did the best you could under the circumstances."
They look at each other. Shirley sighs.

5

Isabel Stamos checks her face in the rearview mirror of her car and waits patiently as a police officer slowly approaches.

"Officer Jennings."

The young man winks and leans against the door of her car. He reaches out to kiss her. Seconds later they're kissing passionately as several cars zoom by. Luke Jennings grins as he pulls away. Isabel slides her fingers across his belt buckle.

"How's your wife?"

Luke rolls his eyes as he watches as Isabel's fingers slide over his swelling erection. She looks at him and smiles slyly.

"I see you're going commando today?"

Luke laughs.

"Got a problem with that?"

"Absolutely not—I think a guy can dress as he pleases. That's how you got me the first time if you recall."

He leers at her.

"I pulled you over for speeding and one thing led to another—best part of my job—scoring with wayward girls."

They look at each other for a few seconds.

"Especially ones experienced at sensual blowjobs."

Isabel watches as Luke unzips his pants and laughs as his penis springs out at her. He grins broadly as she mouths him.

"Need lots of tongue action."

Several minutes later Isabel lets his penis slip out of her mouth and makes a lewd gesture with her finger. She sighs.

"All my friends rave about you."

Luke laughs loudly.

"Tell Natalie and Zabrina I said hi."

Isabel nods.

"I heard you wife is pregnant?"

Luke shakes his head.

Page **47**

"She's due in two months."
Isabel strokes Luke's penis for a few seconds.
"Does she know about me?"
Luke laughs as he rolls his eyes in a mocking way.
"She's on a need-to-know basis."
He kisses Isabel again.
"My shift ends in two hours."
He passionately kisses her again and begins laughing.
"How about you and I meet up later?"
Isabel smirks knowingly.
"Are you planning to take advantage of me?"
Luke grins broadly.
"What do you think?"
He looks at his penis and smirks.

6

"I saw a friend of ours today."
Greg Petrie takes a swig from the mug of beer in his hand.
"Dude still hasn't aged much from college."
Colin Barclay sighs loudly.
"Let me guess who this could be?"
He rolls his eyes.
"Maxwell Pendergraft."
Greg smirks as Colin grabs a handful of assorted nuts from a silver tray nearby. He waves his hand around and gags.
"Bet you anything he's still popular."
Greg seems upset.
"His dad is confined to a care home facility."
He swallows another mouthful of beer. He waves his hand in the air seconds later. He seems irritated as he gestures.
"Carson Penney really did a slick number on poor Orville Pendergraft—evil bastard used his power to defy the law."
Colin looks at the nuts in his hand.
"Eventually scumbags like Penney get their due."
Greg nods and slaps Colin on the back.

Page **48**

"Hopefully sooner than later in this case if there's any justice left in the world. Garbage like Penney and his son are the reason this country is so fucked up. It's time to change the game to favor the little guy again and not types that abuse power."

Greg nods in agreement.

"That's exactly what Maxwell said earlier."

He looks at the empty beer mug.

"He said his father's new lawyer is already putting the skids on Penney and his son—but didn't give a lot of details."

He makes an angry gesture with his hand.

7

Chandler glances at Ivy's battered body and shrugs as he looks down at the ravine. He glances at Castle Beach in a distance and smiles broadly as he carelessly pushes Ivy's body over the edge. As the corpse tumbles into the shrubbery he smirks.

"Out of sight is certainly out of mind."

He hears a rustling sound behind him and turns around but sees nothing. He sighs loudly and begins to walk away.

"I think I'll call Susan Lancaster."

He begins to laugh.

"I guess it's time for me to make new friends."

He hears a crackling sound a few feet away and turns to look where the noise is coming from. As he watches with a mixture of curiosity and fear, a man slowly approaches him. He seems in a trance as the black-clad figure comes into view. Chandler blinks as he notices the old-fashioned clothing the man is wearing. The eerie figure stops a few feet away without looking directly at Chandler and for a second or two, there is silence.

"Hey dude, Halloween is months away."

He seems annoyed that the figure doesn't respond but takes a step forward. Chandler shrugs as he backs away.

"Terrible fashion statement if you must know, buddy."

He mockingly rolls his eyes and smirks.

"Who let you out of the house dressed like that?"

As Chandler watches, the black-clad figure turns to face him directly. The first thing noticed are the eyes and then the shiny teeth protruding from the mouth of the oddly-dressed man. An eerie stillness envelops the area they look at each other. A few seconds pass and Chandler realizes the black-clad figure is inches away from him now. He slowly backs away but to no avail.

"What the fuck are you?"

Chandler is unable to look away from the glowing eyes that seem to pierce his soul as he's pulled toward the black-clad figure. Screams are heard as the wind seems to pick up.

8

"Are you seriously asking me how many of your friends I've bedded in the last month since you and I first hooked up?"

Isabel nods and kisses Luke.

"Give me details."

Luke laughs as he seductively strokes Isabel's hair.

"I'm a sexually active guy—end of story."

Isabel pushes Luke away suddenly.

"What happens if you impregnates one if us?"

Luke kisses Isabel and winks slyly.

"I'll pay for the abortion of course."

He laughs.

"It's the least I can do."

Isabel slides her fingers across Luke's chest and smiles.

"When exactly did you lose your virginity?"

Luke looks at Isabel curiously.

"I don't remember—eight grade perhaps."

He pulls Isabel under him as the bed squeaks loudly. He grins as her attention seems totally focused on pleasing him.

"You're on the pill, right?"

Isabel nods.

"It's not like I have choices at the moment. My much older boyfriend refuses to wear a condom when he fucks me."

Luke grins broadly.

"I told you before it would be too suspicious to explain to my wife why I have a package of condoms in my pocket."

Isabel rolls her eyes.

"Ugh—your wife is a total bitch. I bet you anything she got pregnant just to snag someone like you all for herself."

They kiss passionately.

"Why don't you tell her she's a bore?"

"I can't. I thought I told you already. Her old man is a nutjob. He'd skin me alive if he knew I was dallying with you."

Isabel reacts as Luke penetrates her.

"But just so you know I'm quite fond of you and your friends. The last couple of weeks have been most enjoyable in case you didn't know. Most twenty-six year old guys I know never get to fuck hot high school girls—it's been quite a thrill."

Isabel sighs as Luke ejaculates.

"Do you think anyone knows about us?"

Luke looks at Isabel curiously.

9

"They lost everything during the Great Depression. Several killed themselves. Last one died in Boston I think."

Parker looks at Wendy as she leans forward and whispers in his ear. He seems shocked at what he's hearing. He sighs.

"But who would do something like that?"

Wendy shrugs.

"No one knows what happened exactly. The place fell into ruin during the 1960s. One day in 1966 it caught fire. Rumors spread all over town that the place was being used as a sex commune and somehow one of the hippies that lived there started a fire and burned the entire estate to the ground. Nothing left standing except the front steps from the main house."

Parker gives Wendy a cautious look.

"What about the cemetery? Why didn't anyone move the bodies buried on the estate? Move them to a new cemetery?"

Wendy waves her hand in the air.

"The estate became badly overgrown and pretty much forgotten by everyone in Castle Beach. I hope Chris changed his mind about breaking into the mausoleum—before things."

Parker looks at Wendy oddly.

"Maybe I should go back?"

Wendy grabs Parker's arm seemingly upset.

"Wait until morning—promise me."

Parker notices the terrified look on Wendy's face.

"What—why?"

Wendy glances at the empty diner.

"I heard a while back that the place is haunted."

Parker seems about to laugh as Wendy shoots him a curious look and whispers in his ear once more. He reacts.

"I don't believe in stuff like that."

Wendy sighs loudly.

"Not believing doesn't mean it's not possible. Please heed my warning. Besides, the place has all sorts of dangerous insects crawling about looking for prey—best to wait until morning."

"New England has poisonous insects?"

Wendy is about to reply when the front door opens and she sees Clyde entering with Shirley. Upon seeing him her face lights up. Parker notices and grins broadly at the scene.

"Go talk to your boyfriend. I'll wait."

"He's not my boyfriend."

Parker grins slyly.

"Uh-huh—whatever works for you."

Wendy shakes her finger at Parker and then joins Clyde and Shirley at the far end of the tiny diner. Parker watches the interaction between them for a few seconds and smirks.

"Someone needs to play cupid."

Wendy and Clyde share a brief glance at each other as Shirley picks up a menu tucked into a blue plastic holder. A few other people enter the diner at that moment and Wendy goes over to warmly greet them at the door. Shirley looks at Clyde.

"How long is this going to play out?"

Clyde seems confused.

"What are you talking about?"
Shirley glances at where Wendy is standing.
"When are you going to ask her out?"
Clyde seems embarrassed.
"We're just friends."
Shirley glances at Wendy again.
"She likes you."
Clyde blushes at the remark and shrugs.
"I'm much too old to think about things like that."
"Says who?"
Clyde looks at Wendy again.
"She and Robert were married for thirty years."
Shirley rolls her eyes.
"I know he'd want her to be happy."
"But what if she says no?"
Shirley smirks.
"She won't."
Clyde seems uneasy.

10

"Damn, you've got to be the luckiest guy in Castle Beach by far. You've fucked just about every girl from our school—some more than once according to rumors swirling over various social media sites. No one can even come close to your record."

David Sherwood grins broadly at the compliment and shoves Kyle Webster lightly as they walk down the street.

"So I've played hard—big deal."

He sighs loudly.

"Nevertheless Susan Lancaster has proven to be quite a challenge. First time I've ever had to be patient with a girl."

He laughs.

"But I'll get her. Bet on it."

Kyle looks at David with admiration.

"Exactly how are you going to score with Susan?"

David winks slyly.

Page **53**

"I'll promise to remain faithful."

Kyle begins laughing.

"Who's dumb enough to believe a line like that?"

He sticks his finger in his mouth.

"That scheme is going to get you nowhere."

"My dick is quite charming if I do say so myself. Banged every girl I wanted to in the last year and a half. Except for Susan I've never been told no. If it wasn't for Chandler Penney pursuing Susan I would've scored already. She seems to think he's some kind of nice guy. Thinks he really likes her. Ugh—gross."

"You told her about what he did right?"

David makes another lewd gesture with his finger.

"I did. Not that it seemed to matter to her that Penney left Orville Pendergraft to die by the side of Pickwick Highway."

He seems upset at the idea and stops suddenly.

"Chandler Penney is a scumbag."

He wipes sweat from his brow.

"If I could just get him alone for a few seconds I'd break his frigging neck in several places and then watch him slowly die."

He laughs as Kyle reacts to his statement.

"I would. I swear I would. No one would care either. Except maybe his father—who's worse than Chandler by the way."

Kyle gives David an odd look and nods.

11

Shadows play across the well-manicured cemetery as two men skulk across the headstones in a rush toward a free-standing mausoleum a few yards away. Seconds later the sound of glass being broken can be heard as the stained glass windows of the mausoleum are hit with a hammer. A few minutes later they leave as quietly as they came. Loud laughter can be heard as they drive off. The eerie stillness of the night returns immediately except for the annoying chirping of crickets and other nocturnal insects beginning their nightly prowl for a temporary mate.

12

"Wonder what's going on there?"

Kirk Wheeling pulls up alongside a car parked at the edge of a road and waits a few minutes as he nervously taps his fingers on the steering wheel. He glances at his watch and sighs.

"Probably nothing—just two horny teenagers doing what teenagers do—but I still have to bust them both regardless."

He steps out of his patrol car and slowly walks toward the car. He notices some scuff marks on the dirt surrounding the area where the car is parked. He stops briefly and looks closer.

"This looks like Chandler Penney's car?"

He turns to look back at his patrol car a few feet away.

"Better set him on the straight and narrow."

From the corner of his eye he sees a dark shape sticking out from the other side of the car. He pulls out his gun and slowly walks around the car and stares in shock at the scene. Chandler is lying on his back in the dirt, eyes wide open, a look of terror etched on his face. Kirk seems in shock for a few minutes as he looks at the body before him. He pulls out his cell phone.

13

Megan Bowers looks at the number flashing on her cell phone repeatedly and sighs loudly. She tosses the cell phone on the sofa and seems annoyed as she walks into the kitchen.

"She's got some nerve to call me."

At that moment she hears Malcolm pounding on the front door yelling at her. She glances at the phone as the pounding continues. The noise is followed by a string of vulgar profanities as several threats are made. Megan grabs the cell phone and begins dialing as she walks to the door. The knocking stops suddenly. A second or two later Malcolm starts yelling again.

"The cops are on their way Malcolm."

Malcolm kicks the door from the other side.

"I'm going to kill you, *bitch.*"

Page **55**

The door trembles against the blows.

"No one messes with me and gets away with it."

The door is kicked again.

"You're a fucking cunt and I'm going to end you."

He kicks the door again as Megan sees flashing lights outside from the street. A few seconds later she hears what appears to be someone on a loudspeaker telling Malcolm to step away or else. She hears him cursing her repeatedly as he pounds on the door again demanding she open it. As she stands there listening to Malcolm's drunken ranting, she hears the porch suddenly filled with voices. There is a scuffle and then silence. A few minutes later there is a knock on the door. She remains silent until the voice on the other side assures her everything is OK.

"Megan Bowers?"

Megan stands at the door for a moment and then slowly opens the door. She stares blankly at Rodney Bellingham.

"Are you OK?"

Megan nods.

"He threatened to kill me."

Rodney nods.

"I'm taking him down to the station."

He pulls out a card from his pocket and gives it to her.

"Call me tomorrow morning. You can decide if you want to press charges then. I'll be handling your case directly."

Megan nods in agreement.

14

"Your wife needs to treat you with more respect."

Luke glances at Isabel as he dresses.

"I agree."

He leans over to kiss Isabel.

"How about you—do you respect me?"

Isabel pulls Luke down on the bed and grins.

"I'm still thinking about it."

Luke laughs and strokes Isabel's hair.

Page 56

"I'm a sensitive guy with feelings."

He stands up.

"I still remember the first time I got you."

Luke looks at himself in the mirror as he continues talking while Isabel pulls the covers off her naked body. He reacts.

"You teased me repeatedly for a week."

He grins broadly.

"But then it happened. You spread your legs and left nothing to my imagination—made it easy for me to play."

He leans over and slyly slides his finger into her vagina as Isabel seems to revel in the control she has over Luke.

15
Boston

"I warned you not to defy me and you did anyway. Next time the stained glass windows won't be the only thing damaged. Hope you loved your wife. It would be such a terrible insult if her casket ended up in the middle of traffic on the freeway."

Jeremy Winterfield grins broadly as he listens to loud yells on the other end of the line. He rolls his eyes and sighs.

"Enough with the dramatics Penney—like I told you, if you come up against me again I'll be forced to remove your wife's casket from the vault at Rolling Meadows and drop it in the middle of rush hour traffic and see how many times it can be hit by passing cars and trucks before dear sweet Mrs. Penney spills out of that gaudy fifty thousand dollar gold-covered casket."

There is a pause on the line.

"Forget about going to the cops about this sad matter. It would be a shame if your Russian deal got exposed publicly."

Jeremy laughs loudly.

"Well, that and the fact I've got every cop from this area in my pocket. It's not looking good for you Penney. Better heed my warning before things really become terribly unpleasant."

Jeremy begins laughing as he shuts off his cell phone and props his feet up on the top of his desk. He smirks slyly.

"That reminds me. Got to get in touch with my friends at the local news media—might be interesting if I feed them a story about Penney Associates and possible overseas business deals which have been denied until of late. Shake things up a bit."

He snaps his fingers and begins dialing.

16

"No signs of trauma whatsoever."
Kirk seems confused as Emma Jahnston turns to face him.
"Young Mr. Penney seems to have just expired."
Emma pulls a sheet over Chandler's face.
"I'll know more when I complete an autopsy."
Kirk runs his fingers through his hair.
"When will that be?"
Emma shrugs.
"Day after tomorrow is a good guess."
Kirk and Emma walk toward the steel doors at the end of the sparsely furnished room. He stops and looks back at the sheet-covered body and seems upset. He shakes his head.
"I guess I should call Carson Penney."
He pulls out his cell phone.

17

Parker watches as Wendy comes toward him with a huge smile on her face. He gives her a sly look which she ignores.
"Did you ask him out?"
Wendy pretends to slap Parker playfully.
"I did no such thing."
Parker grins.
"I can play Cupid if you want me to?"
Wendy seems shocked.
"Don't you dare say a word to Clyde Walker about any of what we talked about—I forbid it. Leave it alone. *I mean it.*"
Parker lazily rolls his eyes and winks slyly.

"I'll think about it."
Wendy glances at Clyde and Shirley.
"Not one word."
"Not tonight anyway."
Wendy shoots Parker a cautious look and sighs.
"Not ever."
Parker looks over at Clyde and Shirley.
"I can't make such promises."
Wendy leans over the counter and whispers.
"If you insist on playing Cupid I'll fix you up with Louise Winkler. I have it on good authority she's sweet on you."
Parker seems shocked.
"Hey—that's just plain cruel."
"Oh well."
Parker has a terrified look on his face.

18

Rodney leans back in his chair as he looks at his cell phone. He glances at the paperwork on his desk nervously.
"This just happened?"
He stands up.
"OK—I'll check it out myself personally."
He shakes his head.
"Some people have too much time on their hands."
He heads to the door.

19

Kirk slowly steps out of his patrol car and slowly begins walking toward the front entrance of the Penney mansion.

20

Natalie Cassell looks at Neil Wainsright with disdain as he shoots her a dirty look while he reaches for the doorknob.

"I'll call you tomorrow."
Natalie walks over to where he is standing.
"I don't like you having a girlfriend."
Neil grins.
"I wasn't aware I needed your approval."
Natalie rolls her eyes.
"Justine Ross says that the two of you are exclusive."
Neil laughs.
"She can believe what she wants."
He pulls Natalie toward him and kisses her.
"I do what I want when I want."
Natalie giggles.
"I guess that explains your college tutor?"
Neil grins broadly.
"Uh-huh—Jill Stevens and I are quite friendly."
Natalie pushes Neil away.
"You men are all dogs."
Neil pulls Natalie toward him again.
"Does that include Officer Jennings also?"
Natalie reacts.

21

Luke grins broadly as he starts the engine of his car and drives away from the hotel parking lot. As he drives along a deserted stretch of road he notices a man dressed entirely in black walking aimlessly—zigzagging every now and then.
"Seems like he's had quite a bit to drink?"
He pulls over and slowly steps out of the car.
"Hey you—mind if we chat a bit?"
There is a moment of silence between them and then the black-clad man turns around to face Luke. Immediately Luke is mesmerized by the yellow glowing eyes and is unable to take another step. An eerie silence befalls the area as the black-clad figure takes a step forward. His sharp teeth gleam wickedly.
"Is this some sort of prank?"

He watches as the strange figure slowly approaches.
"What's with the eyes buddy?"
As the darkness enfolds him, Luke screams.

22

"I'll call you tomorrow to meet with my lawyer."
Shirley nods and reaches out to hug Clyde as she seems about to cry. He hugs her again and turns to walk away.
"It'll be all right. Don't worry."
She watches him go.
"How could I have let this happen?"
She wipes a tear from her eye.
"He believed in me and I let him down."
She begins to cry.

23

Carson Penney looks at the face of his dead son as Emma and Kirk watch from afar. As he strokes Chandler's cheek he seems to become enraged. He turns to face Emma and Kirk.
"He just up and died?"
Emma takes a step forward.
"Until I complete an autopsy it seems so."
Carson turns to face Kirk.
"My boy didn't just up and die. He was murdered."
Kirk and Emma share a glance.
"If your son was murdered we will know soon enough."
Carson looks at his son's corpse once more.
"I want whoever did this to be punished."
He reaches out to touch Chandler's face again.
"I'll crucify the bastard."
He looks at Emma and Kirk one more time and then storms out of the room in a rage. They look at each other.
"What if he wasn't murdered?"
Emma seems nervous as she looks at the door.

Page 61

24

Rodney looks at the broken stained glass windows fronting the damaged mausoleum and shakes his head. He looks back at his patrol car as George Fisher comes toward him.

"Got all the shots we need. I'll give you a copy first thing in the morning. The insurance guys are just gonna love this."

They look at each other.

"Kids are probably responsible for tonight's activities—bet they won't like the punishment coming once we get the results on the fingerprints we lifted from around the property."

Rodney nods.

"Anyone called Carson Penney yet?"

George shakes his head.

"Number was busy when I tried a few minutes ago."

Rodney turns to look at the mausoleum again.

"I'm so glad I don't have kids."

He sighs loudly.

25

Parker closes the door behind him and seems stunned to see his mother standing in the doorway looking at him.

"Is something wrong?"

Abigail Ross looks at the cell phone in her hand for a few seconds and then faces Parker. She seems visibly upset.

"Do you know where Chris is?"

Parker shakes his head with a nervous twinge.

"I haven't seen him since earlier today."

His mother looks at him curiously.

"No one has seen him for several hours."

"Maybe he went to the mall?"

Abigail shakes her head. She seems confused as her eyes dart around the empty room nervously. She wrings her hands.

"The mall is closed. It closed about an hour ago."

Parker twitches a little as he turns and walks toward his room. His mother looks at the cell phone in her hand again.

26

Carson drives through the gates of his Victorian-era mansion and notices a lone police car parked in front. He angrily steps out of his car with a look of raging anger on his face.

"What are you doing here?"

"It seems some kids were at the cemetery earlier."

Carson shrugs.

"Get off my property."

Rodney looks at Carson oddly.

"The windows of your family's mausoleum at Rolling Meadows were blown out earlier by some troubled kids."

Carson looks at mansion in front of him and back at Rodney. He clenches his fists in anger and begins cursing.

27

The darkness of night enfolds the front lawn and the shrubs surrounding the small building attached to the main police department that doubles as a jail. Malcolm stares out the window as he watches what seems to be a black-clad figure moving across the lawn. He blinks a few times and sighs. But each time he opens his eyes the dark figure appears to get closer.

"What the hell is that?"

Suddenly the black-clad figure looks directly at him with glowing eyes. He tries to look away but can't. He blinks again.

"Where the fuck did that thing go?"

He turns around and tries to scream but no sound comes out of his mouth. The black-clad figure is in the cell with him. He tries to move but seems frozen in shock as a ghastly white hand grabs him by the collar and pins him against the wall. He watches in terror as the mouth of the dark-clad being opens to reveal very sharp white teeth. Darkness engulfs him two minutes later.

Page **63**

28

"I plan to do terrible things when I catch you."

"You have to catch me first."

Mark Relling grins as he begins jogging faster while his girlfriend Ingrid Mifflin passes him along the side of the road.

"I swear by my threat just so you know."

Ingrid looks back and grins broadly.

"I'll hold you to it."

As she turns the curve she notices a car parked by the side of the road. As she gets closer she stops suddenly and begins screaming. Mark catches up with her and looks in shock at what she's looking at. A man's body is lying propped up against the hood. They take a step forward in unison. Ingrid seems to recognize the man as she comes within a few feet of the car.

"It's Officer Jennings."

Mark looks at Ingrid curiously.

"You know him?"

Ingrid nods still in shock.

"Sort of—he gave me a ticket about a month ago and tried to pick me up. Asked me out on a date but I told him I had a boyfriend already—didn't much like being rejected as I recall."

Mark seems upset at the revelation.

"Is this the first time I'm hearing this story?"

Ingrid ignores Mark and reaches out to touch the body.

29

Parker pulls up in front of David's house and waits a few minutes before the teen comes out. In the backseat is Preston Sago with a laptop tapping away silently. David gets into the car and slams the door shut. They look at each other briefly.

"Still no word on your cousin?"

Parker shrugs.

"I think I know where he might be."

David looks at Preston curiously and then at Parker.

"Did you kill your cousin?"

Parker gives David a dirty look.

"Chopped his head off to see what would happen."

He seems worried as he drives away.

"I warned him."

He sighs.

"But he didn't want to listen."

David and Preston look at Parker for a second.

"We went to a cemetery near Pickwick Highway yesterday afternoon. Chris was talking about some old treasure map."

"What cemetery? There's no cemetery out there—just some old creepy estate that burned to the ground way back in the 1960s. Some deal about a bunch of sex-crazed druggie geeks."

"There *is* a cemetery. I saw it yesterday."

David turns to look at Preston.

"This is what happens when you don't get laid enough. You get yourself in trouble by skulking around creepy old estates with abandoned houses. Like seriously, I mean, really?"

He turns to face Parker again.

"What exactly happened yesterday with you and your stupid cousin? Why would you even go by a place like that?"

Parker shakes his head.

"Chris wouldn't take no for an answer."

"What else in new when it comes to you and your stupid cousin—exactly what did you do that you shouldn't have?"

"Like I said earlier, Chris and I trespassed into the old Nix estate and then broke into the mausoleum at the cemetery."

"When did you two dummies get back to town?"

Parker shrugs and looks at David nervously.

"We didn't. I left Chris at the mausoleum and hitched back to town. I haven't seen or heard from him since yesterday."

David runs his fingers through his hair.

Kirk looks at the tray in his hands as he slowly walks down the hallway toward a row of jail cells several feet ahead.

"Got some grub for you Kingsbury."

He looks at the tray once more and then at the first cell a few seconds later. He drops the tray in shock. Malcolm is lying on the floor—his eyes wide open. Kirk fumbles with the keys as he hastily opens the cell door. He looks down at Malcolm's dead body unsure of what to do next. He pulls out his cell phone.

31

Natalie sighs loudly as she looks at the pregnancy kit on top of the sink and then at herself in the mirror. She seems in a panic as she tosses the kit into the trash nearby. She shrugs.

"What am I going to do?"

She gasps.

"Is it Neil's or Luke's?"

She looks at herself in the mirror again.

32

Ingrid and Mark watches as Luke's body is placed inside a coroner's van. They glance at Emma talking with someone from the State Police. A coroner's assistant shuts the door and walks toward the front. Mark hugs Ingrid tightly and sighs loudly.

"Probably had a heart attack while driving?"

Ingrid shakes her head several times in a confused way.

"He's a young man—mid-twenties I think."

Mark glances again at Emma talking to one of the officers a few feet away as their conversation gets really heated.

"She seems pretty upset about something."

Ingrid glances at the police car nervously and sighs.

"His body felt really strange."

Mark shrugs and looks at Ingrid curiously.

"His body felt strange?"

"When I touched him earlier he wasn't cold."

Mark spins Ingrid around to face him.

"Maybe he wasn't dead that long when we found him?"

Ingrid shakes her head.

"I heard Emma say to her assistant that Luke has been dead approximately six hours. Rigor mortis would have already set in for a body dead that long. But that can't be possible."

Mark turns to look at Emma briefly.

"Maybe we should go home?"

Ingrid pulls away from Mark and sighs.

33

Carson angrily throws a vase toward a window as he looks up at a huge matte oil painting of Chandler. As the vase crumbles around his feet—he pounds the wall with his bare fists until they are bloodied. Carson finally stops and begins sobbing loudly.

TO BE CONTINUED

A Brief Look at the Third Episode

A small town in New England falls under a cloud of darkness as events from the past haunts the present while several teenagers attempt to figure out what happened to one of their own.

Episode 3
Wonderland

1

Milton Donovan shrugs as he listens while Greg Petrie talks on his cell phone. A few seconds later Greg shuts off the phone and turns to face Milton. He seems unable to speak.

"What did your friend at the police station say?"

Greg wipes sweat from his brow.

"Chandler Penney is dead."

Milton reacts in shock at the news.

"What?"

Greg leans back in his chair.

"Luke Jennings is dead too—as is Malcolm Kingsbury."

Greg stands up.

"They just found Malcolm in his cell—dead. I was told he was brought in last night for threatening Megan Bowers."

Milton seems confused.

"Did he kill himself?"

Greg shakes his head erratically.

"Malcolm was just dead—no cause outright."

He seems upset and makes a gesture with his hand.

Page **69**

"No signs of trauma to the body whatsoever."
He rubs his neck with his right hand.
"Same deal on Chandler's and Luke's body apparently."
"How is that possible?"
Milton watches as Greg rubs his chin.
"No idea."
Greg waves his hand in the air.
"Chris Gibson and Ivy Patterson are missing also."
Milton seems troubled by the recent turn of events and nervously taps his fingers on the desk for several seconds.
"This happened late last night?"
Greg nods and runs his fingers through his hair.
"I'm going to pay Emma Jahnston a visit."
Milton looks at the folder in his hand.
"What about Jessica Sago's apprenticeship?"
Greg stops and turns around.
"Tell her to meet me back here after lunch and we'll chat."
"Thanks."
Greg looks at his watch.
"Lock the door behind you when you leave."
Milton nods.
"No problem."
He watches Greg leave.

2

"Still think he's at the mausoleum?"
Parker Ross nods.
"It's as good a place as any to start looking."
David Sherwood rolls his eyes as he steps out of the car and turns to face Preston Sago and Kyle Webster. They look at the overgrown path leading into the thick growth of thorny shrubs and stop. They seem uneasy about venturing further.
"Did you see any spiders?"
Parker turns to face David with a smirk.
"What do you think?"

Page 70

David glances back at his car.

"I hate spiders."

Preston and Kyle laugh loudly and point at David.

"Oh-oh—should we get a pacifier for you?"

David reaches out to grab Preston who pulls away.

"Oh, like real funny virgin boy."

Preston seems stung by the comment.

"Cruel move Sherwood."

David grins broadly.

"It is what it is."

He turns to face Parker.

"OK—I know I'm going to regret this but let's go see that cemetery you said is out there in the woods. By the way when I find Chris I'm going to kick his ass for being so moronic."

Parker waves his hand and leads the way into the thick underbrush a few yards away from where they parked.

3

"I never thought this could happen to me?"

Natalie Cassell looks at Zabrina Relling and shrugs.

"I thought the pill always worked."

Zabrina rolls her eyes.

"Did you forget to take it?"

Natalie sighs loudly.

"A couple of times last month I think."

Zabrina shakes her finger at Natalie and smirks.

"Picked out names yet?"

Natalie seems shocked at the comment.

"You're not helping."

Zabrina laughs.

"Do you know who the father might be?"

Natalie seems about to cry.

"Luke or Neil I guess?"

Zabrina reacts.

"What about David or Casey?"

Page **71**

Natalie shakes her head.

"David and I slept together only one time."

She seems upset.

"Casey Sago dropped me last month because of Neil."

Zabrina smirks and makes a lewd gesture with her finger.

"Oh, that's right, I remember. He caught you and Neil playing doctor in the backseat of your car. Pissed him off that his hated arch rival on the football team was banging his girl."

Natalie pretends to slap Zabrina.

"Neil and I are just friends with benefits."

Zabrina rolls her eyes again.

"What about Officer Jennings?"

Natalie laughs.

"He's a happily married man."

Zabrina makes another lewd gesture with her finger.

"Tell his penis that."

Natalie looks down at her stomach.

"I wish Officer Jennings was the father without a doubt. I know that he's married but I don't care. He's so good-looking."

Zabrina winks.

"He and I hooked-up the day before yesterday in his patrol car. He was an animal the whole time—blew his load twice."

Zabrina looks at Natalie oddly.

"I'm glad we decided to share him."

Natalie waves her hand.

"I had no decision in the matter. He made it clear to me when we fucked for the first time that I was just one of many."

She looks down at her stomach again.

"But I love him regardless."

They hear a noise behind them and turn to see Jessica Sago standing a few feet away. She seems upset and sighs.

"Have you guys heard?"

Natalie and Zabrina look at Jessica slightly confused.

"Heard what?"

Jessica sits down next to them.

"Chris Gibson and Ivy Patterson are missing."

She leans closer to them.

"Chief Wheeling and his team are searching for them as we speak. Their parents are freaking out royally I heard."

She begins whispering.

"Chandler Penney is dead and so is Malcolm Kingsbury according to what a friend of mine who temps at the morgue told me. Oh, and someone else told me Officer Jennings was found dead this morning. Not a mark on him from what they said when they found the body. It's really strange if you ask me."

Natalie seems about to faint.

4

"Not a mark on any of them?"

Emma Jahnston nods as Greg looks at her and shrugs.

"But how can that be possible?"

Emma shakes her head.

"People die all the time and sometimes there is never a real reason as to why. They just die and that's it. It happens."

Greg nervously runs his fingers through his hair.

"But in a small town like Castle Beach?"

Emma glances at the hallway in front of her.

"I'll know more about what happened to them after I complete their autopsies. Right now I'm drawing a blank."

Greg looks at his watch.

"Any word on the whereabouts of Chris and Ivy yet?"

Emma shakes her head again.

"No."

Greg glances at the steel doors at the end of the hallway.

"Can I get a peek?"

Emma gives Greg a curious look.

"I'm afraid not."

Greg looks at the hallway once more.

"OK—but I want details when the autopsies are done."

Emma looks away.

"I'll think about it and let you know."

Greg grins broadly.

"How did Carson Penney react to the news?"

Emma waves her hand in the air.

"How do you think he reacted to finding out his eldest son was dead? Penney was crushed—seemed about to snap."

Greg shuts off his digital recorder and shrugs.

"I guess now he knows how it feels to suffer a loss."

Emma has a shocked look on her face.

5

"Not one more step guys."

David, Parker, Preston, and Kyle slowly turn around to see Rodney Bellingham looking at them from his patrol car.

"Go back to town this instant."

David rolls his eyes.

"Must you always be a total drag Bellingham?"

Rodney steps out of the patrol car.

"Want to say that to my face Sherwood?"

They look at each other.

"This entire area is under investigation as of now."

David and Parker look at each other.

"But Chris might be?"

Rodney shakes his head.

"I'm going to count to ten and if by then you guys aren't on your way back to Castle Beach—I'll make sure you all have splendid accommodations at the police station tonight."

David gives Rodney a harsh stare.

"No wonder my sister ditched you for Milton Donovan."

Rodney stares at David as he points to their car.

"Be gone this instant or else."

They file past him and silently get into their car. As they drive off he looks at the thick growth of shrubs just ahead.

"Where did they think they were going?"

He shakes his head and faces his patrol car.

"Chandler Penney is dead?"

Jeremy Winterfield leans back in his chair as he continues to talk on his cell phone. He shakes his head several times.

"OK—just keep me updated on the details. This really puts a crimp in my plans to screw Penney to the wall. Fuck it."

He stands up and shakes his fist in the air.

"You know what—I don't care. Serve that sick bastard the paperwork anyway. Tell him I don't give a fuck that his freak show of a son is on a slab in the morgue. He's going to pay regardless of these turn of events or I'll turn his life into a scary nightmare."

He shuts off the cell phone.

"Heartless troll you are."

Jeremy turns around to see Andrew Latimer looking at him with a mixture of shock and admiration. He grins broadly.

"Carson Penney is getting what he so richly deserves for how he's treated everyone he's ever known over the years."

"Remind me never to piss you off."

Jeremy smirks.

"What can I do for you today?"

Andrew hands him a folder and grimaces.

"It seems like Roger Segrino has run afoul of Webly Oil yet again—he's been threatened with a multi-million dollar suit."

Jeremy looks at Andrew curiously.

"Is that so—seems Webly Oil should be worried right about now. Call Segrino and tell him I'm taking the case."

He laughs.

"Then start looking for dirt on Webly Oil and don't stop until you find something I can use to bury those bastards."

Andrew grins and turns to walk to the door. He stops.

"Just so you know I really appreciate being your assistant for the last two years. Seeing you destroy morally corrupt people is quite a thrill—especially knowing they rightly deserve it."

Jeremy takes a bow in front of Andrew.

7

"Can you believe that guy?"

David angrily pounds his fist on the dashboard of Parker's car while Kyle and Preston shake their heads knowingly as they drive toward the highway. Cars zip by them a few at a time.

"Fucking prick times two."

He clenches his fists tightly.

"He's really asking for a wallop no doubt."

Preston rolls his eyes.

"What do we do now?"

Parker looks at his watch and shrugs.

"Maybe there's another way into the cemetery?"

David seems confused.

"Why don't we just forget this stupid cemetery expedition and face reality OK? Dumbass Chris probably hitched a ride with some sleazy old dude who has a thing for teenage guys."

Parker turns to look at David.

8

"Thanks for getting me an apprenticeship with the *Daily Spill*. I really appreciate it. I won't let you down. I promise."

Milton looks at Jessica and smirks.

"Hey, sometimes having friends in the right places isn't such a bad thing Jessica. But it's still on you to do the work."

Jessica looks at the cell phone in her hand.

"I'll do my best."

Milton glances at his watch.

"I've got to go—but don't forget what I told you."

Jessica nods.

"I won't. I promise."

She watches him go and turns to look at her cell phone again. She begins flipping through a roll of photographs taken around Castle Beach. She sighs loudly as she stares at a photo of

Page **76**

Malcolm Kingsbury hugging her at a family picnic the summer before. Jessica shuts off her cell phone and stares blankly at it for a minute or two. She wipes a tear from her eye and shrugs.

"I can't believe he's dead."

She wipes another tear from her eye.

"He was so young."

She sighs loudly.

"He had so much to live for."

She looks at the cell phone again.

9

Carson Penney looks at the young man dressed in Levi's and a T-shirt. He seems about to explode as he grabs the folder and angrily throws it at the front entrance of his mansion.

"How dare you show up with this trash?"

Barry Fowler sighs.

"I'm just doing my job sir."

He looks at the folder lying on the steps.

"That said—you should be aware that Winterfield and Associates are going ahead with what was started before your son met such an unfortunate ending yesterday evening."

Carson grabs Barry by the neck.

"Get out of my sight you disgusting ghoul."

Barry jerks free from Carson's grip and looks at the folder lying on the steps again. He tries to pick it up but Carson stops him and wrings his arm backwards. Barry takes a swing at Carson with his other arm and knocks him down into the nearby shrubbery. Carson reacts in shock. Barry grabs the folder from the step and throws it at Carson, looking at him with contempt.

"If I were you I'd lawyer up right away."

He notices looks at the sky overheard and grins.

"Have a nice day."

As Barry walks away Carson pulls himself out of the shrubs and storms into his mansion—slamming the front door shut.

Page 77

10

Kirk Wheeling closes the front door to the police station as Rodney looks up from his desk. They stare at each other for a few seconds as Kirk notices Rodney's annoyed look. He sighs.

"It's been quite a day."

He slowly walks toward his desk.

"Can this day get any worse?"

Rodney leans back in his chair and smirks.

"David Sherwood and his friends were up to no good earlier this morning. I caught them trespassing by the old Nix estate. They seemed pretty gung ho about going into the woods for some reason. Sherwood actually seemed ready for a fight."

Kirk rolls his eyes and sits down.

"Young Mr. Sherwood better stay on the straight and narrow if he knows what's good for him. Castle Beach has all the problems it can handle at the moment. According to Emma Jahnston there were no signs of trauma on any of the bodies."

He shrugs.

"Tomorrow can't come soon enough."

Rodney glances through the window toward the building next door and stands up abruptly. He walks over to Kirk's desk.

"What if the autopsies don't tell us anything about why Luke and the others expired? What then? Just asking?"

Kirk runs his fingers through his hair.

"Have their medical records been sent to Jahnston?"

Rodney shrugs.

"I assume."

"Any word yet on Chris and Ivy?"

Kirk seems worried as he shakes his head.

11

"I thought you said you were an athlete?"

Juliet Sago watches as her boyfriend Ethan Polzoni finally catches up to where she's standing. He stops suddenly.

"I was. But age has crept up on me."

Juliet rolls her eyes knowingly and looks at the view in a distance. She feels some loose gravel under her feet and looks at the scuff marks on the ground. She turns to look at Ethan.

"This must be where they found that kid."

Ethan doesn't answer. She notices his gaze and follows it as her eyes catch sight of something blue in the shrubs below the bluffs. Juliet takes a step forward. Ethan grabs her arm.

"Where do you think you're going?"

"There's something blue down there."

Ethan looks down at where Juliet is pointing.

"It's just trash."

Juliet smirks.

"Someone should pick it up."

She begins to climb down the rocky ledge.

"Be careful."

Juliet turns to look back at Ethan and waves as she makes her way further down the rock-covered hillside. As she gets closer she sees a hand sticking out of the shrubbery and screams.

12

"Chris wasn't kidnapped by some sex fiend."

Parker turns to look at David with disgust. He glances at Kyle and Preston as they shake their heads. He sighs loudly.

"He probably fell inside the mausoleum."

David rolls his eyes.

"Why hasn't he called for help?"

"Maybe he can't."

He turns to look at Kyle and Preston again.

"I say we go back."

David waves his hand in the air.

"Party pooper Bellingham might have something to say about that. Dude is a serious prick—totally a wet blanket."

He clenches his fists.

"I want a piece of him really bad."

Parker stifles a snicker.

"Exactly why did you sister dump Officer Bellingham?"

David turns away from Parker.

"She said he was overly cautious or something. I think it was because he was too dull for her. My sister is not a wallflower by any means. She likes to have fun. Last year she went on a trip to Iceland by herself. Said it was the best thing she ever did."

Parker stifles another snicker.

"Isn't that where she got pregnant?"

David turns to look at Parker with a scowl.

"If you're insinuating for any reason that my sister slept with some random dude from Iceland I'll bust your face."

Parker pulls over by the side of the road.

"If not some dude from Iceland—then who's the daddy?"

Without warning David slugs Parker.

"My sister is not a whore."

Parker begins laughing as he rubs his shoulder.

"I never said she was—chill out OK?"

David seems ready to hit Parker again.

13

Natalie looks at a photograph of Luke Jennings and begins to cry softly. She glances at her stomach and seems nervous.

"What am I going to do?"

She traces her finger over the photograph several times.

"He was so sweet."

She looks at the photograph again.

"He would've been such a wonderful father to my baby."

She looks at the front entrance of her house.

"How do I tell my parents?"

She looks at the photo again and sighs. She slips it into her pocket and looks at the house once more. She shrugs.

"Maybe I won't have to tell them anything?"

She slides her fingers across her stomach and pauses for a few seconds before walking up the slanted driveway.

Page **80**

14

Juliet and Ethan watch as a covered body is loaded into a coroner's van. Kirk glances at Juliet and Ethan as he talks with Emma and then comes toward them. Juliet seems uneasy.

"Who could do that to someone?"

Kirk shrugs and gestures.

"Lots of sick people out there unfortunately."

Kirk walks toward the edge of the bluff and looks over.

15

"Thanks Emma."

Greg leans back in his chair as he faces Jessica sitting a few feet away. He seems lost in thought for a second or two.

"Ivy Patterson is dead."

Jessica reacts as Greg stands up.

"They just found her body a few yards from where they found Chandler Penney earlier. She was pretty busted up."

Greg notices Jessica's reaction to Ivy's death.

"Did you know Ivy?"

Jessica shakes her head.

"I met her a few times. She attended Pinecrest Prep."

She stands up.

"You said her body was busted up?"

"Uh-huh—pretty badly from what Emma said."

He sighs loudly.

"Her parents will be devastated."

He glances at his cell phone.

"Ivy's been found but Chris Gibson is still missing."

Jessica looks at Greg curiously.

"You don't think?"

Greg shrugs.

"Do I think Chris killed Ivy?"

He picks up his cell phone and faces Jessica.

Page **81**

"No—he has been missing since yesterday afternoon. Ivy was seen last night with Chandler in his car—around eight."

Jessica watches as Greg jumps up and runs to the door. He stops suddenly and turns around to face her. He seems excited as he stands there motionless—lost in thought for some reason.

"It would all make sense."

"What would?"

Greg glances at his cell phone and pauses for a few seconds. Suddenly his fingers fly across the screen as he furiously dials. He faces Jessica with a glint of mischief in his eye.

"What if Chandler killed Ivy?"

He glances at the front door.

"*But how did he die?*"

They look at each other.

16
Boston

"I'm aware of the recent turn of events. Regardless, the suit is still moving ahead. Your father will be compensated."

Jeremy smirks.

"He's already been served."

He laughs.

"He was fit to be tied from what I was told."

He leans back in his chair.

"People like Penney hate it when they're not the ones in control since they assume the world revolves around them."

Jeremy grins as he lets his fingers dance across the desktop. He nods a few times and snaps his fingers twice.

"Within a week he'll settle with you."

He glances at the paperwork in front of him.

17

"You didn't have to hit me earlier?"

Parker watches as David steps out of the car.

Page **82**

"You called my sister a whore."

Parker rolls his eyes and gives David a knowing look as he glances at the deserted street up ahead. He shrugs.

"She had a baby with some dude she hardly knew."

David's face turns bright red.

"Would you have respected her more if she'd gotten an abortion like so many other women do? Seriously, judging people on fake religious standards set by other people is something that only those morally-challenged loser pundits from FOX News excel at despite the fact they have so many skeletons in their own closets. My sister isn't perfect but at least she's not a two-faced hypocrite—which by the way is far worse than being a liar."

He leans against Parker's car.

"I'm also perfectly willing to admit I'm not flawless by any means. I'm certainly not boyfriend material given how many girls I'm slept with *and* I could be a better friend to everyone in Castle Beach. But at least I'm willing to admit it and not pretend I'm someone I'm not. How many people do you know who are willing to admit and face their shortcomings? Let me know when you come across someone like that. I'm all ears when you do."

He taps Parker on the shoulder.

"I'm really sorry about what happened earlier. I shouldn't have hit you. You just pissed me off royally and I reacted."

Parker shakes his head and smirks.

"Don't worry about it."

He looks at David's house.

"I'll call you tomorrow."

David nods and glances at his cell phone and sees several words flashing by. He turns to look at Parker once more.

"They found Ivy Patterson—*she's dead.*"

Parker reacts to the news.

"Something is afoot—and not in a good way."

David looks at his house.

"Call me when you get back home."

Parker nods in agreement.

18
Night

Natalie paces back and forth for several minutes and then walks toward the window. She sighs loudly as she looks out toward the front lawn of her home. She pulls out her cell phone and begins dialing. A few seconds tick by as she waits. Natalie glances at the lawn again as the inky blackness of night begin to dance joyfully. Shadows seem to pop up everywhere as Natalie notices something slowly moving in the darkness. She shrugs.

"Is someone out there?"

She turns away from the window.

"It's probably just some stupid animal."

Natalie looks at the cell phone again and finally shuts it off. She seems upset as she throws it on the bed nearby.

"Where is she?"

She looks back at the window and then sits down on the edge of her bed. She strokes her stomach lightly and sighs.

"What am I going to do?"

There is a scratching sound at the window and as Natalie turns around to look she sees Luke Jennings standing on the other side of the window. She jumps up and runs toward the window as a huge smile spreads across her face. Luke's fingers rap on the window pane again as she comes closer. They look at each other for a few seconds. Luke looks at the latch and motions for her to open it. She hastily opens it as Luke grins broadly.

"You can't stay long—my parents would freak."

Luke glides into the room and circles Natalie as she looks at him strangely. She notices his teeth and then his eyes. She seems unable to move as Luke embraces her—and without warning he bites her on the neck. She tries to scream but no sounds come out of her mouth as Luke hungrily feeds. Every few seconds he looks at her and laughs and then resumes drinking as she seems in shock over what is happening. Outside the window a silent hush comes over the area. Not a sound can be heard.

19

Parker throws his cell phone on his bed and notices a picture frame on top of his dresser and sighs. He walks over and picks up the silver-capped frame and stares at it briefly.

"Where are you Chris?"

He looks at the picture of the two of them standing in front of a rocky beach. He slowly places the picture frame back on top of the dresser and walks to the window. He looks out.

20

Neil Wainsright grins as Zabrina hastily unzips his Levi's and slides her hand into his underwear. He laughs loudly.

"Still think I'm a dog?"

Zabrina looks at Neil curiously.

"I'm OK with it actually."

Neil smirks.

"Justine thinks I'm studying with a friend tonight."

Zabrina pulls Neil's jeans down to his knees and looks at his erection straining against the confines of his boxer briefs.

"She's a really dumb girl."

Neil laughs.

"Uh-huh—I agree. Not too fast on the draw."

He makes a lewd gesture with his finger and smirks.

"But she gives really good blowjobs."

Zabrina pulls Neil's boxer briefs down and stares at his exposed penis. He winks at her as she kisses the head several times. Seconds later his penis disappears inside her mouth. On a desk a few feet away her cell phone continues to flash.

21

Megan Bowers turns around every few seconds as she slowly walks down the dimly-lit hallway inside her house.

"No reason to get freaked out tonight."

Page **85**

She walks into the kitchen and pulls out a key. As she puts the key into the lock for the back door she hears a sound. She nervously turns around and looks at the hallway. No one is there. She focuses again as she begins to open the back door. She hears another sound and turns around slowly. At the end of the hallway a figure is bathed in darkness. She panics and furiously attempts to open the door. A cold hand falls on her shoulder a second later. She turns to see Malcolm Kingsbury looking at her with a grin on his face. His sharp teeth gleam in the shadowy light as she seems drawn to his glowing eyes. She screams only one time.

22

Susan Lancaster waves goodbye and watches as a car pulls out of view. She turns to walk toward her house and stops. A few yards away in the nearby shrubbery a slight movement in the shadows catches her attention. She stands motionless as she peers into the darkness—but sees nothing. She turns away and walks up the front steps. There is another sound. She stops and turns around again. Her eyes dart back and forth in the darkness but still there is nothing to see. She shakes her head and opens the door. As she enters she glances once more toward the area where the sounds came. Eerie silence fills the chilly night air.

"It's just a cat on its nightly hunt."

A few feet away she hears a loud snap and at that moment she quickly shuts the front door and bolts it. She pulls the drapes over all the windows in the living room. Her eyes wide with fear as the sounds increase. She pulls out her cell phone.

23

"What is happening in this town?"

Parker nervously looks out the window of his bedroom.

"Where the hell could Chris be?"

He hears a knock on the door and a voice.

"I need to talk to you."

Page **86**

Parker turns away from the window and walks to the door and opens it. Justine Ross looks at him curiously seeing the odd expression on his face. He slowly motions for her to come into the room and as he closes the door he turns around to face her with a blank look. She snaps her fingers several times in front of his face as he finally seems to acknowledge her. Justine rolls her eyes.

"What's up with you?"

Parker shakes his head.

"Nothing's up with me. What do you want?"

Justine looks at Parker curiously.

"I think Neil is playing me."

Parker laughs.

"I told you that over a month ago."

Justine rolls her eyes again.

"That was then—but this is now."

Parker sits down on the edge of his bed.

"Neil Wainsright is a louse. It's been common knowledge among everyone in Castle Beach for years now. He's almost as bad as Chandler Penney was except he's got no money."

Justine sticks her finger in her mouth.

"Ugh—don't ever mention the name Chandler Penney to me again. He tried to put the moves on me at Neil's birthday party last week. Said he would change me forever. Like ugh."

Justine sits down next to Parker.

"I know I've been nasty to you lately. But I really need guy advice when it comes to Neil. Should I break up with him?"

"You need to do what's right for you."

Justine rolls her eyes and seems upset and pretends to slap her brother as he moves out of the way. She sighs loudly.

"That's no answer."

"It's the only one I've got."

He turns to face his sister again with a serious look.

"Wainsright is a sleazy creep. He uses people. But it's your choice whether or not you want to stop being with him."

He flips his middle finger.

"This is what I think of Neil Wainsright."

Justine gently shoves her brother.

"OK—OK. I get your drift. You hate the guy."

"Uh-huh—with good reason."

"I guess you're right—which isn't very often."

Parker puts his arms around Justine and hugs her warmly as she kisses her brother on the cheek. He feigns disgust.

"Oh-oh—so you like me now?"

"Of course I like you—we're siblings aren't we?"

Parker grins slyly.

"I heard mom say you were adopted."

Justine jabs her brother with her finger and laughs.

24

Susan screams as she looks at Chandler Penney on the other side of the huge bay window. His fingers slide across the glass pane several times as she looks at him curiously. His yellow eyes glow with intensity as he looks at her, his focus clearly on her exposed neck. He grins broadly and knocks on the window again as Susan seems to realize what's happening. She turns away from the window and glances at a small gold cross on top of her jewelry case. She walks over to it. The scratching continues to get louder and more insistent as whatever is outside seems intent on getting into her bedroom. She faces the window again and walks toward Chandler who seems to be floating in mid-air. She slyly hides the cross behind her back and when she's within four feet of the window, pulls it out and points it at Chandler. Upon seeing it he hisses angrily, throwing up his hands in front of his face.

"Go away."

Susan continues to hold the cross in front of her as Chandler's earlier grin disappears and is replaced by a hateful glare as he slowly backs away from the window. Within seconds the area outside the window is again blanketed by darkness.

"What the hell was that?"

She continues looking at the window.

25

Rodney stands motionless in the parking lot looking at the man approaching him. He blinks several times not sure he's seeing what's coming at him. The old-fashioned clothing sticks out in Rodney's mind as the man comes closer. Rodney lets his hand slide down to the holster where his gun is kept. He sighs.

"Can I help you?"

The figure approaching him doesn't respond.

"Hello?"

There is no answer.

"Hello? I asked you a question?"

The figure looks directly at him and Rodney immediately is drawn to the glowing yellow eyes. He's unable to look away as Thomas Nix comes closer. Suddenly Rodney is held in the grip of the man wearing old-fashioned clothes. He offers no resistance as his neck is punctured by sharp white teeth. From that moment onward there is utter silence except for sucking sounds.

26

Neil grins broadly as he waves to Zabrina and walks down the driveway of her home to where his car is parked. As she closes the front door the entire area is engulfed in darkness. A second or two later he hears a snap and turns around. Nothing is there. He reaches out to open the door of his car as a loud snap is heard nearby. He turns again to look but sees nothing. He shrugs.

"I've really got to get a grip before I freak."

He gets into the car and presses the ignition. As he guns the engine he feels a presence next to him and screams.

"How the fuck did you get in my car?"

Luke grins broadly as he stares blankly at Neil.

"Wait—aren't you?"

Before he can react Luke embraces him. Neil screams in terror. Outside the loud chirping of insects can be heard.

Page **89**

Parker hugs Justine once more and then closes the door to his bedroom. He runs his fingers through his hair and sighs.

"Neil Wainsright."

He sits down on the edge of the bed.

"I hate that guy with a passion—certainly wouldn't mind it one bit if someone took him out—justifiable homicide."

He glances at his cell phone lying on his bed and is about to pick it up when he hears a scratching sound. He turns around and stares in shock at the window. Outside Chris Gibson is looking at him with a curious mixture of joy and hunger. Parker rubs his eyes and looks at the window once more. Chris raps on the window and points to the latch as Parker seems confused.

"Chris? Where have you been?"

The entity outside the windows doesn't respond except to rap on the window again. Parker seems to realize what Chris has become and blinks several times in rapid succession in order to avoid the mesmerizing stare from Chris. He finally stands and looks directly at the window. Chris seems to be floating back and forth as he continues to scratch at the window. Parker scans his room for a religious artifact and spots a small statue on a corner table at the far end of his room. He walks over to it. As he does, the noise outside increases as Chris seems to want to change the course of events unfolding. Parker grabs the statue and faces Chris. As the statue is pointed directly at Chris he reacts.

"I'm really sorry Chris."

He looks at the statue and smiles as it seems to have achieved some semblance of power in his hands. He grins.

"Who knew?"

Parker watches as the thing outside his window that resembled Chris throws its arms over its face and disappears from view. Seconds later the scene in front of him is gone like it never happened. Parker looks at the statue in his hand and then at the window for a few seconds. He seems unsure of what to do.

"How did Chris become? Is he?"

He sits down on the bed once more and glances at his cell phone. He picks it up and begins dialing as he looks at the window again expecting to see Chris hovering in mid-air.

"I must be dreaming."

He shakes his head several times.

28

David rolls his eyes as he listens to Parker on the phone yelling at him. He looks toward the window and shrugs.

"Dude, you're acting really crazy."

David shrugs.

"Just tell me what the deal is already? Why do you want me to pull all the drapes? What the hell is going on? Spill it."

He sighs loudly and seems frustrated.

"OK—OK—I'll do it. But tomorrow you better start making sense when we meet. I'm not in the mood for your games."

He nods a few times and then shuts off his cell phone. He casually throws it on the bed and glances at the window.

"What's his issue with the windows?"

He walks over and begins pulling the drapes shut.

"What's the deal with everyone tonight?"

He looks at his watch.

"First Susan calls and tells me she saw something at her window but wouldn't tell me what. Then Parker insists I pull all my drapes. This is beginning to feel like a really bad movie."

He wrings his hands several times.

"Except I'm in *this* movie—and the freaks are my friends who have apparently lost their minds. Is it possible Parker and Susan are pulling my leg—trying to get a rise out of me?"

He looks around the room briefly and quickly heads to the door still not sure he will do what he was instructed to do.

"This is really going to go over well with the folks when they ask me why I'm shutting out the view of Pine Street."

He sighs as he opens his bedroom door.

29

Lisa Morgan rubs her eyes as the scratching continues and looks toward the window. Outside she sees Malcolm looking at her and pointing at the window. She seems confused as she climbs out of bed and slowly walks toward the window as if she's still asleep. She looks at Malcolm curiously, noticing some sort of reddish stain on his shirt collar. His gaze seems to be looking past her for a few seconds and then he faces her directly. His eyes glow with a yellowish hue that strikes her as odd. She tries to look away but is unable. She watches as he indicates for her to open the window and as she slowly moves closer toward the window she seems to realize something. She stops and looks around.

"Dead—they said he was dead?"

She looks toward the window again as the glowing eyes staring directly at her seems to rid her of every fear she could possibly have at the moment. The insistent scratching continues as she carelessly ignores sensible caution over the possible danger whatever is outside poses to her and opens the window slowly. Malcolm grins broadly—showing her very sharp teeth. As he approaches Lisa his eagerness is obvious. Seconds later he embraces her and begins to feed. As he drinks Lisa gives into whatever is happening to her and doesn't offer much resistance as her life slowly ebbs away and slips into inky darkness.

30

Carson looks at his watch and seems lost in thought as he notices the stack of paperwork in front of him. He stands up.

"That ghoul Winterfield won't get one red cent from me despite what he thinks. I'm through giving away money."

He turns to look at the paperwork again.

"Chandler was my shining star. He was going to make me proud—carry the Penney name into the next four decades."

He rubs his eyes.

"He was the perfect son."

Page **92**

He shrugs and is about to leave the room when he hears a loud knock and turns to see Chandler standing outside.

"What's Chandler doing outside?"

He watches curiously as Chandler's finger slides across the glass pane. He shakes his head a few times as if to wake up but each time the scratching sounds only get louder. He sighs.

"Chandler? Is it really you?"

As Carson watches, the thing outside the window nods endlessly as if to hasten their encounter. Carson seems unsure of what he's seeing but nevertheless continues to acknowledge the eager demands coming from the other side of the window.

"But you can't be?"

The loud scratching becomes more demanding while Carson proves unable to deny what is expected of him from the entity resembling his son. He reaches out and begins unlatching the window as if under command. As the window is opened the room fills with a cloud-like vapor while father and "son" look at each other. Chandler grins at Carson as he's drawn closer and closer to the entity standing before him unable to break his stare. As time seems to slip by Chandler embraces his father and drinks hungrily. Loud screams are heard before utter silence.

TO BE CONTINUED

A Brief Look at Fourth Episode

A band of brave teens sets out to exterminate an ancient evil that seems intent on destroying Castle Beach one person at a time as townspeople seem oblivious to the awakening nightmare.

Shadow Dancers

1

Shirley Brewster stands silently as she looks at the man on the other side of the window looking at her. His eyes glow with a determined intensity as he makes a gesture for her to open the window and let him inside. She seems unable to move as the man seems to dance back and forth—almost gliding mid-air. She tries to look away as he becomes more insistent while his fingers rap against the glass pane. She finally gives in to the demands from the oddly-dressed man and opens the window. Within a second he embraces her and his razor-sharp teeth sink into her neck.

2

Marlisa Turner rolls her eyes and turns to look at the empty parking lot ahead of her. She looks at her watch and sighs loudly as she walks toward her car about ten feet away.

"They could've waited."

She fumbles through her purse looking for her keys as shadows begin to dance toward her from the inky darkness.

"Ungrateful wretches they are."

She hears a noise and looks up to see Luke Jennings looking at her with a curious grin on his face. His lips seem to be covered in some red substance. She watches as he edges closer to her. She begins to back away and stops suddenly. Behind her she sees Malcolm Kingsbury. He and Luke look at each other and nod in unison. For the first time she notices their glowing eyes and sharp teeth. She tries to run but it does no good. Seconds later they both attack her like a pack of wild animals and begin feeding, hungrily tearing at both sides of her neck as she screams for help. Her screams subside almost instantly as loud laughter echoes throughout the parking lot amid sucking sounds.

3

Wendy Emerson closes the door to her diner and begins walking down the street. From behind her she hears footsteps but sees no one when she turns around. She begins walking faster and as she turns the corner she catches a glimpse of Chris Gibson following her about six feet away. She immediately notices his eyes and teeth—before screaming in panic. She runs down the sidewalk as if being chased by her worst nightmare. As she turns the next corner she sees Juliet Sago about to get into her car and calls out to her. Seconds later she slams the door shut and turns to look at Juliet. Her eyes are round as saucers. She sighs.

"Nightmares are coming to life."

She looks over her shoulder and then at Juliet.

"*Let's get out of here*—I'll explain later."

Juliet sighs and begins driving away as Chris stops. A look of rage seems to spread across his face and he hisses loudly.

4

Melora Schubb walks slowly down the hallway of the Penney mansion and stops in front of the den. She sighs.

"Is someone in here? Mr. Penney?"

Page **96**

She slowly enters and notices splatters of blood on the floor and some of the furniture. As her eyes continue to look at the bloody scene she sees Carson Penney lying on the floor about twenty feet away. There is blood everywhere. She screams.

5

Juliet pulls into the driveway of Wendy's home and shuts off the engine. She turns to face Wendy. Wendy keeps looking back as if expecting to see someone standing behind the car.

"OK—what's going on?"

Wendy faces Juliet and shrugs.

"I saw someone—Chris Gibson to be exact."

Juliet looks at Wendy oddly.

"Isn't he missing?"

Wendy nods.

"Something was wrong with his eyes."

She looks back once more as if still expecting to see Chris right behind the car. There is nothing there but darkness. Juliet slowly reaches out to touch Wendy's hand. She seems worried.

"Is there someone you want me to call Wendy?"

Wendy pulls her hand away.

"I know what I saw."

Juliet shakes her head.

"I don't know what to tell you."

Wendy looks up at her house and sighs.

6

Kirk Wheeling looks at the bloody scene in front of him and at Melora. Her eyes dart back and forth between the bloody spots on the floor and Carson's body. She sighs loudly.

"Who would want to hurt Mr. Penney?"

Kirk glances at Carson's body once more and shrugs.

"Did you see anyone on the property earlier?"

Melora shakes her head multiple times.

Page **97**

"You stated that you came downstairs to get a glass of milk and saw the door of the den open—and then you found Carson lying on the floor? Is that what you saw Melora?"

Melora nods.

"Yes."

Kirk looks at the window.

"Was the window open when you came downstairs?"

Melora shrugs.

"I'm not sure."

They look at each other.

"I gather the Penney children are away at boarding school at the moment? Are there any other people on the property?"

Melora glances at the door.

"John Weddleton. He's the Penney groundskeeper. He has his own separate quarters out by the other end of the estate."

Kirk looks at Carson's body again.

"I'm going to pay him a visit. In the meantime do not touch anything in here until I call the coroner. Is that clear?"

Melora nods several times.

7

Juliet pulls up in front of the driveway of her home and steps out of the car. The area is oddly silent as she begins walking toward the back door. As she walks past several large bushes she hears a noise and as she turns around she sees Chris looking at her from a few feet away. She screams only once before he attacks her—his teeth ripping at her throat. As he begins to drink in a frenzied rush silence seems to envelop the area instantly.

8

Susan Lancaster listens as loud scratching sounds continues outside the window. She looks at the crucifix in her hand and begins to repeat prayers as time slowly ticks by.

"Morning can't come soon enough."

Page **98**

As she continues to look at the drapes nervously the scratching stops but resumes a few seconds later. Susan looks at the crucifix once more and shrugs as she begins praying.

9

Kirk knocks several times on the wooden door of a small guest house. There is no answer. He tries the doorknob and as it gently opens he sees John Weddleton lying on the floor near a coffee table. He seems unhurt but nevertheless dead. Kirk notices a few droplets of blood on the sofa and on the floor nearby.

"What the hell is going on in Castle Beach?"

He pulls out his cell phone.

10

Morning

The light of the early morning rays begin to sparkle as a new day begins in Castle Beach. A few joggers venture out for a morning run as abandoned cars are noticed parked on various side streets. Spots of blood can be seen on some of the cars.

11

Kirk walks through the steel doors of the morgue. In the middle of the room the covered bodies of John and Carson lie side by side. Kirk shakes his head as he slowly turns to face the assistant deputy coroner with a look of worry on his face.

"Not a scratch on either of them."

"Quite troubling about Emma Jahnston as well—can't locate her at all. Her cell just keeps going to voice mail."

Kirk shakes his head.

"She's nowhere to be found?"

"I stopped by her home earlier—she wasn't there."

Jim Tyner walks over to the covered bodies. Kirk watches as he pulls the sheet away covering John Weddleton's corpse.

"No marks whatsoever on either of the remains—not even a pinprick. With the exception of the bloody clothing—clean."

Kirk seems confused and sighs.

"You mentioned something about the others?"

Jim runs his fingers through his hair.

"Several bodies are missing."

"You're pulling my leg right?"

Jim shoots Kirk an odd look and sighs.

"Do I look like I'm playing a prank?"

Kirk looks at the sparsely-furnished room as Jim walks toward the far end of the room and points to one of the vaults.

"The only corpse we have is that of Ivy Patterson."

He sighs loudly.

"Sometime last night someone broke into the morgue and apparently stole the remains belonging to Chandler Penney, Malcolm Kingsbury and Luke Jennings. I should note that I found nothing wrong with the lock. It's just very odd—very odd."

Kirk shakes his head and shrugs.

"The tabloids are going to have a field day."

He seems uneasy and sighs.

"What if Emma Jahnston took the bodies last night?"

"No way would she be involved in something so heinous. I've known her all my life and she's rigid as they come where rules are concerned. This has nothing to do with her whatsoever."

Kirk walks toward the door.

"I'm going to look at the security cameras."

Jim nods several times.

12

Ethan Polzoni looks at Kirk nervously as he walks into the police station and stops halfway in the middle of the lobby.

"Can I help you Polzoni?"

Ethan seems unsure as he walks toward Kirk.

"Juliet is missing."

Kirk seems confused.

Page 100

"Maybe she went to the market?"

Ethan rolls his eyes.

"She didn't come home last night."

He sighs loudly.

"I thought maybe she was with a friend and lost track of time. But this morning when I woke up she was still not back. Her car is in the driveway but she's nowhere to be found."

Kirk runs his fingers through his hair.

"Did you check with her friends?"

Ethan nods and looks back at the door nervously.

"They haven't seen her either."

Kirk stands up.

"Let's go."

They leave the police station in a rush.

13

"I've told that boy so many times not to leave his car in my driveway. But does that blockhead ever listen to me? No."

Zachary Relling glances back at his house and then again at the car in his driveway. He notices Zabrina standing at the front door. He seems annoyed as he faces her directly.

"I thought you promised me that dumbass boyfriend of yours wouldn't spend the night? I thought I made that clear?"

Zabrina walks toward her father.

"Neil didn't spend the night. He left about ten."

Zachary rolls his eyes.

"Then what is his car doing in my driveway?"

Zabrina shrugs.

"I don't know daddy."

She watches as her father walks toward Neil's car and begins pounding on the window. Zachary glances with disdain at Neil Wainsright for a few seconds and turns to face Zabrina.

"Your blockheaded boyfriend is drunk as a skunk."

Zabrina seems shocked at the statement.

"Neil doesn't drink daddy."

Page **101**

"Well, he certainly looks zonked out of his mind."

Zabrina walks towards Neil's car. She seems cautious as her father continues to ramble on about Neil's behavior.

"I'm calling his parents right now."

Zabrina turns to face her father and reacts.

"Wait—something's wrong—he—he's—*oh my God.*"

Zabrina looks at Neil sitting upright in the driver's seat. As she realizes the horrible truth she begins screaming loudly.

14

Wendy stands outside her diner and seems hesitant to open the front door. She finally opens it cautiously and slowly ventures inside just as Clyde Walker comes up behind her.

"Wendy?"

Wendy turns around and seems in shock as she looks at Clyde. He notices her reaction as he stares at her. She watches as he glances toward the parking lot nearby. He sighs loudly.

"Is everything OK?"

She shakes his head.

"Something happened to me last night."

Clyde looks at Wendy curiously. She notices.

"Let's go inside and talk."

He follows her inside and as she shuts the door she peeks to make sure no one is in the vicinity. Clyde watches as Wendy turns to face him again. She wrings her hands several times.

15

Kirk follows Ethan towards Juliet's car. Ethan stops as Kirk looks at the area. Hardly any sounds can be heard. He sighs and turns to look at the car again. Ethan's eyes nervously dart back and forth as if he expects Juliet to show up at any moment.

"Where could she be?"

Ethan watches as Kirk tries the locked door.

"There has to be an explanation."

Page **102**

He glances toward the shrubbery nearby and slowly approaches the stylishly cut plants as Ethan follows. As Kirk approaches the bushes he notices a spark of yellow and as he looks closer he realizes it's a shoe. As Ethan watches from a few feet away, Kirk slowly pulls some of the low-hanging shrubs out of the way and sees Juliet. She appears to be sound asleep but as Kirk reaches out to touch her body he realizes she's dead.

16

"It's time to get up Natalie."

Clarissa Cassell knocks on the bedroom door again. She seems annoyed as she stands silently for a few seconds.

"Enough is enough."

She opens the door and reacts as she sees her daughter lying on the bed staring upwards. Her eyes are wide open. Natalie Cassell seems oddly peaceful as her mother reaches out to touch her daughter's body and realizes the truth. A second later she flees the room screaming as she runs toward the stairs.

17
Ten Minutes Later

David Sherwood pulls on a T-shirt as he opens the front door of his home and sees Susan standing on the front steps.

"OK—spill the details about last night."

Susan glances at David nervously and turns to look at the street. Several cars drive by as she faces David once more.

"Let's go somewhere and talk."

David follows Susan to her car and watches as she keeps looking around nervously as if expecting someone to jump out at her. David reaches out to grab her arm. He seems upset.

"Spill the drama already. I heard enough crap from Parker last night. He's playing the same game you are—wouldn't tell me over the phone what happened. This wanabee *Grimm* storyline is really getting tired if you must know. I'm not at all amused."

Page **103**

Susan steps into her car and motions for David to do the same. He gets in and slams the door shut. He looks at her.

"OK—what's up?"

Susan stares at David for a few seconds.

"I saw Chandler Penney last night."

David stifles a snicker.

"Yeah, right—uh-huh—I'll just bet you did."

Susan nods.

"He was at my window."

David rolls his eyes in a mocking way.

"This is what you wanted to talk to me about?"

Susan grabs David's arm.

"He was outside my window. He looked really weird."

David laughs loudly.

"Of course he looks weird—the dude is dead."

Susan grips David's arm tightly. He notices and tries to pull away as she tightens her grip. She seems about to cry.

"He was just hovering outside my window. He seemed to be floating or something. His eyes—they were yellow—they were glowing—and he seemed to have some reddish substance on his shirt as well. He had really sharp teeth too. It was so freaky."

Susan releases her grip on David's arm.

"Don't you think I know this sounds totally nuts."

David rolls his eyes and smirks.

"As opposed to what you already told me just minutes ago? If you're going to tell me that bastard Penney faked his own death so he can play games with us—I'm not buying it."

Susan seems uneasy.

"What if he's not dead? But undead?"

David seems about to burst out laughing.

"*Salem's Lot* this isn't."

Susan's face turns bright red.

"I'm not fooling around David. I think Chandler Penney is a vampire. There's no other way to explain what I saw last night at my window. It was freakish—ghastly actually—totally unreal."

David gestures with his hand.

"I told you years ago to stop watching reruns of *Buffy the Vampire Slayer* and the 1990s version of *Dark Shadows*. This is what happens when you start thinking old TV shows are real."

At that moment they hear a honk and see Parker Ross staring at them from his car. David rolls his eyes and sighs.

18

"I'll be there as soon as I can. I'm shorthanded at the moment. Whatever you do don't touch anything. OK?"

Kirk faces Ethan as he slowly shuts off his cell phone.

"It seems there's been another death in town."

Ethan looks at Kirk confused.

"How did they die?"

Kirk runs his fingers through his hair and shrugs.

"Rodney Bellingham is missing as well."

Ethan reacts to the news.

19

David looks at Parker and Susan curiously as they sit on either side of him on a bench in a park. He shakes his head.

"This whole thing sounds crazy."

Parker suddenly grabs David by the arm.

"I know what I saw last night."

He looks at Susan.

"Her story mirrors mine."

David stifles a smirk.

"Should I call **Sarah Michelle Gellar**?"

"Don't you think we know how whacked this sounds. But we both saw what we did. It was definitely Chandler and Chris that visited us. There's no doubt. They're both vampires."

David jerks free of Parker's grip.

"Even if what you say is true—no sane person will believe us. They'll lock us up in the booby hatch in ten seconds flat."

Susan suddenly stands up and faces David.

"Then it's us against those things."
David looks at Parker.
"What the hell is she talking about Parker?"
Parker shares a glance with Susan and then faces David.
"If Chris is a vampire—then it must have started at the old cemetery he and I visited. Something must have happened to him while he was at the mausoleum or in the woods nearby."
Susan wipes sweat from her brow.
"But how did Chandler?"
David shoots Parker a knowing look and smirks.
"Explain that smart guy."
Parker looks at Susan and David. He shrugs.
"I have no idea."
He sighs.
"We've got to go back to the mausoleum."
Susan looks at Parker oddly.
"I'm not sure that's a good idea."
David and Parker turn to look at Susan.
"Why?"
Susan pulls a strand of hair out of her face.
"What if whatever got Chris is still there waiting—for us?"
Parker grins.
"Then we'll kill whatever is there."
He looks at David.
"How about we go get Preston and Kyle?"
David looks at Susan.
"Well? Is this your deal or not?"
Susan's face instantly clouds over in panic.

20

Zachary wipes his brow and looks at Zabrina.
"Chief Wheeler said he had another case to deal with but would be right over first chance he got—said not to touch anything before he comes here. He sounded rather frazzled."
He glances at the driveway again and sighs.

Page **106**

"Where's your mother?"

Zabrina points toward the house and shrugs.

"I saw her in the laundry room about ten minutes ago."

She turns to look at the house once more.

"I tried reaching Natalie earlier. There was no answer. It's not like her to ignore me. I think something's wrong."

Zachary turns to look at Zabrina with a curious look and then faces Neil again. He shakes his head several times.

"If I didn't know better I'd say he was sleeping—seems quite relaxed for some reason. It's as if he's not really dead."

Zabrina rolls her eyes at the comment.

21

"This is the most whacked story I've ever heard."

Kyle Webster rolls his eyes as he looks at Susan and David and then Parker. Preston Sago remains silent as he appears to be slightly amused by Kyle's reaction. David seems angry.

"OK—here's the deal guys—we can scoff all we want at what we're being told or we can check it out just to be sure."

Kyle and Preston look at each other.

"This is crazy—vampires roaming Castle Beach? Like how are we supposed to take a story like this seriously?"

Susan grabs Kyle's arm.

"It's all true—I'm not making it up."

Preston stifles a smirk as he notices Parker's glare.

"OK—you guys aren't crazy—*we are*. Like we'd have to be insane to actually believe a **Stephen King** novel has come to life and we're just a few steps away from ending up undead."

Kyle begins laughing hysterically.

"Hello guys—*Salem's Lot* isn't real—it's just a story."

He gestures wildly at them and laughs again.

"What's next—a YouTube video with creepy music as we stalk imaginary beings at some broken down mausoleum?"

David turns to look at Susan and Parker.

"What do we need to do first?"

Page **107**

Parker shoots Susan a cautious look.

"Stakes—we need plenty of wooden stakes and a few hammers wouldn't hurt our deal either. Throw in some holy water for good measure. St. Mark's is just up the street if I recall."

Kyle and Preston break out in laughter.

22

"There has to be another explanation."

Clyde glances toward the front door of the diner. Shades are still pulled over the windows. He shakes his head.

"There has to be."

Wendy gestures with her hand.

"I know what I heard."

She taps her fingers lightly on the tabletop.

"Something was outside my window trying to get inside."

She reaches out to touch Clyde's hand.

"Whatever it was—it wasn't easily swayed."

She notices Clyde's facial expression.

"I think I know what was at my window last night. It had to be Chris Gibson. I saw him earlier and he looked weird. His eyes were really creepy looking. Like a bright shade of yellow. He had this really bizarre smirk on his face—almost like a pervert."

Clyde seems confused.

"What if what you heard was a burglar?"

Wendy rolls her eyes mockingly.

"It wasn't a burglar outside my window last night."

She lowers her voice.

"It was something else—something dark."

Clyde leans back in his chair.

"And what would that be Wendy?"

"I can only think of one thing and one thing only."

Clyde looks at Wendy oddly.

"You're not saying what I think you're saying?"

Wendy nods.

"It would explain what I heard."

Page **108**

"Would it?"
Wendy nods again. She seems upset and sighs.
"I know what I heard."
Wendy glances at the door fearfully.

23

"I hope no one we know sees us doing this."
David shoots Kyle a dirty look.
"You're a nerd Kyle—how much worse can your life get?"
Kyle rolls his eyes at David.
"I'm not a nerd—I'm a tech enthusiast."
David gestures with his hand.
"If you say so Kyle—but tech enthusiast in English means nerd regardless. Face it virgin boy—your sad rep is DOA."
Preston jabs David.
"Nerds rule."
"Keep telling yourself that."
At that moment they watch as Parker and Susan come from inside St. Mark's Church with several containers of holy water. They have a nervous look on their face as they slowly come toward the others. Parker glances back at the church.
"Father John had lots of questions."
David looks at Parker.
"You didn't tell him? Did you?"
"Of course not—do I look like a dummy?"
David watches as Parker places the containers in a box and lays it inside the trunk of the car. He seems uneasy.
"This is seriously freaking me out."
Susan reaches out to touch David's hand.
"How do you think I feel?"
She looks at the others and sighs.
"I know what I saw."
David gives her a curious look.
"What if we can't handle what we find? What if we're dealing with something truly horrible? What do we do then?"

Page **109**

Susan shoots him a cautious glance and turns to look in the direction of the abandoned cemetery. She sighs loudly.

<h1 style="text-align:center">24
New York City</h1>

Simon Penney leans back in his chair as his face changes color when he's informed about Carson Penney's death. He glances at the photographs covering the walls of his office and seems annoyed at receiving the call. He shakes his head.

"I'm really sorry Melora, but you know my stance on this issue has not changed in the last ten years. I no longer consider myself related to Uncle Carson. He turned his back on me a long time ago and now things are the way they are. I agree that his death and the death of my cousin is a tragic situation for all involved but I can't—I won't take responsibility for the immediate future of my cousins. I think the best you can do is to call Carson's lawyer and see what he can do concerning the Carson estate and possible guardianship until something can be decided."

Simon stands up.

"I'm really busy right now."

He sighs.

"Check back with me tomorrow."

He looks out the window of his office.

"Again I'm sorry."

He nods and looks at the screen as it goes blank.

"Carson Penney was quite the scumbag extraordinaire even if he was my uncle. Chandler wasn't much better either."

He stifles a smirk.

"I know I should feel bad but I don't."

He slowly walks toward the huge window looking down on Central Park and does a little dance. He begins to laugh.

"I wonder who my uncle pissed off enough that they deemed it a necessity to rub him and Chandler out. I bet it had to do with some business deal gone wrong—probably drugs."

He glances at the photographs on the wall behind him.

Page 110

"That reminds me. *TMZ* ordered a slew of photographs from my shoot yesterday—wouldn't want to disappoint those guys. Especially now knowing I'm not in dear Carson's will."

He grabs his cell phone and begins dialing.

25

"Are you sure Natalie's really dead?"

Claire Cassell fights back tears as she turns to face Daphne Shaw standing several feet away in front of Claire's car.

"Call me later OK? I'm going to work now but please let me know what the coroner says. I'm so sorry about Natalie."

She nods and shuts off her cell phone.

"I can't believe it."

Daphne reaches out to comfort Claire.

"Natalie wasn't exactly my favorite person but I certainly wouldn't wish her dead even though she slept with my ex."

Daphne looks at Claire curiously.

"Did her mother say how Natalie died?"

Claire shakes her head.

"Not really. She just said she died."

Claire looks at the movie theater a few yards away and seems unable to move for a few seconds. She rolls her eyes.

"I really wish I didn't have to work today."

Daphne gestures with her hand.

"Marlisa is probably waiting for us already with one of her stupid lectures about being late. Ugh—I'm so not in the mood to put up with her foul mood swings today. Like kill me now."

Claire nods in agreement as they walk toward the back door from the parking lot. As they walk they notice Marlisa's car parked at an angle a few feet away and look at each other.

"That's odd. She left the door ajar."

Daphne turns to look at the movie theater.

"She probably tied one on last night after work."

Daphne makes a lewd gesture with her finger and laughs.

"I would if I were her—hateful bitch."

They stop as they notice something sticking out from under the left side of the car. Daphne screams. They look in shock as they see Marlisa's body partially hidden under her car.

"I think someone iced her."

Claire seems to be a state of shocked disbelief as Daphne grabs her cell phone. Bright red spots can be seen on the concrete just out of range from where the car is parked. Claire reaches out to hold Daphne's hand as she begins furiously making calls.

26

Kirk watches as the body of Rodney Bellingham is placed into a body bag and zipped up. He turns to face Ethan.

"Same deal as the others. No marks."

He nervously runs his fingers through his hair.

"I think it's time I bring the state medical board into this situation. I think there might be a flu strain in Castle Beach."

"Like Ebola?"

Kirk shakes his head.

"Whatever is happening it's not Ebola. Bodies would have been a wreck after the fact. Everyone so far just seems to be asleep—could possibly be some new strain of the bird flu."

Ethan watches as the coroner drives away.

27
Afternoon

"I thought there would be a trail."

Parker turns to look at Susan and grins.

"This isn't a park."

Susan rolls her eyes as she follows Parker and David through thick thorny bushes. Behind her Kyle and Preston stop every now and then to brush away cobwebs from their clothing and hair. Ahead they notice the silence that permeates the entire area except for gusts of wind that blow through occasionally.

"People lived here before?"

Parker stops and looks at Susan with pity.

"According to Wendy Emerson the Nix family was loaded and had the run of Castle Beach. From what she told me I think they were the ones who founded this town. But then something really bad happened. Then it was all downhill from there."

Kyle rolls his eyes.

"Oh boo hoo—cry me a river already—rich people having a hard time of it. So sad I forgot to care. Screw them all."

Parker peers into the thick shrubbery.

"From the story I heard they lost everything during the Great Depression and then had to get real jobs in Boston."

Kyle snickers.

"How sad—oh wait—I don't care."

He jabs Parker and laughs.

"Seems to me you feel sorry for them?"

Parker stops.

"Wendy said something bad happened in 1790 to one of the Nix heirs—something that over a century later few people knew about. She said it was whispered about for years."

He looks at his watch nervously.

"She said that Thomas Nix was suddenly taken sick on his way back from Boston and when he returned to Castle Beach he died soon after. Rumors swirled that he'd actually contracted some sort of venereal disease while in Boston but his family refused to talk about what happened for over a century."

Parker stops suddenly and sighs.

"Wendy said he was buried in a separate crypt."

David grabs Parker's arm.

"Did you see his coffin that day?"

Parker sighs loudly.

"I left before Chris opened the crypt."

He turns to face the others and then within a few more yards he points toward the cemetery a short distance ahead.

"We better be out of here come nightfall."

He looks around nervously.

"I don't want to run into anything not alive."

As Kyle continues to tease Parker they come to a clearing in the woods and then slowly began walking toward the broken gate fronting an abandoned cemetery. They slowly walk into the cemetery in silence looking around at broken headstones that appear to be over two or three centuries old. Susan stops and looks back toward the woods a few yards away. She turns and follows the others as they reach the entrance to the abandoned mausoleum. Their footsteps echo on the stained marble with a hollow sound. David and Parker look at each other and at the others for a few seconds. They seem nervous. The silence around them is noticeable. The imposing burial structure gives them something to think about as Parker and David push the door leading inside the mausoleum inward. They peek inside.

"The crypt for Thomas Nix is at the far end."

He watches as the others slowly venture inside.

"What if this Thomas Nix chump is a vampire king?"

Parker turns to face Preston.

"Then we take a stand."

He glances at Susan briefly and sighs.

"If Chris and Chandler are undead—they're not alone."

He sighs loudly.

"According to vampire lore that I found on a few Internet sites—the undead rise the next night after being attacked."

He looks toward the sky.

"This mausoleum could be their lair."

Susan reaches out to hold David's hand.

"What if we open the crypt where this Nix dude is buried and find out that he's not a vampire—king or otherwise?"

Parker turns to face the others.

"I have no idea."

Kyle notices the chunks of a broken crucifix lying on the floor of the crypt. He slowly picks up a piece and examines it.

"What else didn't you tell us Parker?"

Parker glances at the large door fronting the crypt.

"I know as much as you guys do."

Kyle rolls his eyes.

Page 114

"Likely story no doubt."

David slides his hand across the stained marble door as the black grime instantly come off onto his fingers. He reacts.

"Ugh—gross."

He looks closely at the cracks bordering the length of the door and faces the others with a look of disgust on his face.

"There has to be a trigger point."

He sighs loudly.

"I feel like I'm in a *Scooby-Doo* rerun."

Kyle and Preston begin to snicker loudly.

"Except for the fact we could all end up dead."

David ignores them and continues feeling along the cracks in the marble until there is a cracking sound. He steps back suddenly and watch as the door to the massive crypt opens.

"No way to turn back the clock now."

As they peer into the pitch black room they see a coffin in the center of the impressive structure. As they stand there they clearly see lying scattered throughout the room on the floor—the bodies of Chris and Malcolm lying near the door—and Luke's body a few feet away. At the other end they see Chandler Penney lying next to the coffin. The little group glances at each other nervously and seem at a loss for words. They enter the crypt.

28
Boston

"What the fuck is going on in that town?"

Jeremy Winterfield shakes his head as he looks at Andrew Latimer. He stands up and walks toward the window and stops almost in a jerk-like motion. He turns to face Andrew.

"Carson Penney can't be dead."

Andrew looks at Jeremy with a blank stare.

"This will make things much more complicated."

He rubs his face several times.

"His frigging estate will be tied up for years."

He angrily clenches his fists and sighs.

"Possibly decades if his lawyers get their way."
He stops directly in front of Andrew.
"I may need to strike a deal with his people if need be."
He rolls his eyes.
"Are you absolutely sure Penney is dead?"
"They found him either late last night or early this morning according to what I was told. Apparently he just up and died. No cause. At least not until after an autopsy is done."
Jeremy shrugs.
"This really blows chunks."
He walks back to his desk and glances at his cell phone.
"Father and son dying so close together—I wonder if there's a story there. Say, like suicide maybe? Leaking such a tawdry story to the media might increase our odds at making his lawyers see things our way—certainly they wouldn't want a scandal about their client all over the supermarket tabloids."
He grins slyly and faces Andrew.

29

Greg Petrie leans back in his chair as he nervously glances at Jessica Sago sitting in front of his desk while he talks on his cell phone briefly. He becomes more and more agitated and sighs.
"OK—thanks the same—appreciate it."
He shuts off his cell phone and sighs loudly.
"What did he say?"
"This one is just like the others."
He looks at his cell phone once more.
"There is something creepy happening in Castle Beach."
He sighs loudly again.
"Yesterday there were three suspicious deaths aside from whatever happened to Ivy Patterson. So far today there are nine deaths that are extremely suspicious. According to Wheeling there were no marks on any of the bodies. They seem perfect in every way except for the simple fact they're dead—and if that's not suspicious enough—Emma Jahnston is missing also."

Jessica stands up.

"What do you think is going on?"

Greg shakes his head.

"I have no idea. Wheeling seemed to be avoiding talking about it in great detail no matter how much I pushed him to clarify his statements—said something curious about not being able to get in contact with Emma before he said he had to go."

At that moment Greg's cell phone rings.

30

"When did you say those guys from the state medical board would be arriving here in Castle Beach from Boston?"

Kirk shrugs and faces the covered bodies again.

"Not sure. But we might need the guys from the CDC to come from Atlanta as well—we won't be able to keep this a secret for much longer—people talk in this town—news spreads."

Jim makes a gesture with his hands.

"I know exactly what you mean."

He laughs.

"My wife has big mouth."

Kirk grins broadly.

"That's my sister you're talking about."

Jim laughs.

"You said it I didn't."

Kirk shoves Jim.

"I can still belt you like when we were kids. Knock a couple of your teeth out. Make you really unattractive to look at."

Jim flexes his muscular arms and grins.

"Uh-huh—I'd like to see you try."

He faces the covered bodies again.

"Any word on what happened to the other three?"

Kirk shakes his head and waves his hand.

"I'm still working on it."

He runs his fingers through his hair.

Page 117

31

Zabrina traces her finger over a photograph of Neil wearing T-shirt and jeans, holding a football. As her fingers trace along his jeans she sighs loudly. She seems about to cry as she slowly pulls her hand away from the photograph and looks at her cell phone lying on the bed a few feet away. Zabrina shrugs.

"He's gone forever."

She wipes a tear from her eye as she turns to look at a photo of herself with Natalie on a desk about ten feet away.

"What's happening in this town?"

She stands up.

"What happened to Natalie and Neil last night?"

She wipes another tear from her eye and walks toward the window. Outside, the streets are void of life. As she stares at the empty sidewalks she begins to cry and drops the photograph.

32

Shadows start to play on the stained glass windows as Preston nervously looks at his watch. He watches as the others slowly walk toward where Chris and Malcolm are lying. Preston seems in shock as he stares blankly at the corpses before him.

"I can't believe they're dead."

Parker jabs him harshly.

"They're not—they're undead."

He turns back to face the others.

"We have to act fast before they wake up."

Preston sighs loudly.

"What do we have to do first?"

Parker shrugs as he faces Preston.

"Each of them gets a stake in the chest."

Susan watches in disgust as Parker opens the bag they brought with them and pulls out several stakes and hands them one each. He turns to look at Chris lying a few feet away.

"We might as well start with him."

At that moment Preston seems about to throw up.

"Will there be blood?"

David rolls his eyes at the comment.

"What do you think?"

He faces Parker again and sighs loudly.

"What happens if one of them wakes up while we're pounding a stake into their chest? Do we stop or what?"

Parker glances at where Chris is lying.

"They all have to be staked."

He looks toward where the coffin is positioned.

"We'll save Thomas Nix for last."

He grabs a hammer from the bag and shrugs.

"There will be more of them tonight."

Susan reacts.

"But I thought?"

Parker glances at the stained glass windows.

"Chris and the others rose last night for the first time—it can be assumed they hunted and made more like themselves."

Susan looks at the stake in her hand.

"I don't think I can do this."

Parker glances at his watch and at the coffin.

"It's either us or them. You decide."

Susan notices a slight movement from the corner of her eye and screams loudly as Chandler slowly opens his eyes.

TO BE CONTINUED

A Brief Look at the Final Episode

Terror seems to be a best friend to all when a daring group of teenagers take matters of mortality into their own hands as nightfall approaches and evil forces stalks them relentlessly.

Last Light of Day

1

David Sherwood and Parker Ross turn around in unison as Susan Lancaster slowly begins backing away from Chandler Penney. His eyes glow bright yellow, rimmed with red. He grins at her, showing sharp teeth. He slowly rises just as David and Parker attack him. David jams the stake into Chandler's chest and as Kyle Webster and Preston Sago watch from a few feet away, Parker begins pounding on the stake. Chandler cries out in pain as the stake penetrates his skin. His unearthly screams echo throughout the mausoleum as Parker's relentless blows on the handmade piece of sharpened wood takes its toll. Blood gushes from where the stake is embedded in Chandler's chest in a messy spray—and then it just happens without any notice to everyone present—it's over instantly—Chandler's screams fade away and his body rapidly turns into a powdery mist that falls around David's feet and covers Parker's hands. David turns to look at the others with a sort of confused look as Parker stands up and slowly glances at where the body of Luke Jennings is lying nearby.

"One down four to go."

Page **121**

Parker walks over to Luke's body and glances at the others standing a few feet away. David takes Susan's hand.

"It'll be over soon."

David kneels down next to Parker alongside Luke's body and as the others watch Parker brings the hammer down on the stake. As the wood pierces Luke's chest—his eyes fly open—the bright yellow is almost bright enough to light up the darkened room. He screams loudly as Parker brings the hammer down endlessly on the stake until it completely penetrates Luke's chest. Sprays of blood stain David and Parker's clothing as they watch Luke's face begins to distort and eventually fall away to dust.

"I wonder how many of them will arise tonight?"

As if to answer Kyle's question—they hear a loud rustling sound and react in horror seeing both Chris Gibson and Malcolm Kingsbury standing directly behind them grinning—showing sharp teeth. Seconds later Chris viciously grabs Preston.

"What do we do now?"

As they watch helplessly Chris rips into Preston's neck like a wild animal as blood splashes against his clothing. He drinks hungrily as they watch not sure what they can do. Immediately Malcolm begins to circle them—his face masked with an evil grin as he prepares for another kill. Suddenly Susan's world changes and she reaches into her jacket pocket and pulls out a bottle of holy water. Before Malcolm can react she throws the holy water at his face. He screams in agony as the impact scars his cheeks. A second later David and Parker react. Parker rams a stake into Malcolm's chest and David begins pounding on it in a blind rage. Loud screams escape from Malcolm's mouth as the wooden stake hits its mark. Seconds later it's over and all that remains is a pile of dust. Everyone looks at each other in shock and then faces Chris. As they react in horror they realize Chris has vanished.

"He's gone."

Dark gloom surrounding them is all that they see. They are alone except for the closed coffin and Preston's limp body.

"Where did he go?"

They look at each other confused.

"Is he? You know?"

David and Kyle turn Preston over and look at the mangled flesh that had been his throat less than ten minutes before.

"Is Preston?"

Kyle turns to look at Susan and shakes his head.

"He's dead."

She begins sobbing loudly.

2

"Are you sure it's Shirley Brewster?"

Clyde Walker watches Kirk Wheeling nodding as they walk down the hallway toward the morgue. He stops and sighs.

"It's her—I'm sorry. We just need to confirm it."

Clyde nods and watches as Kirk pushes the door to the morgue inward and they enter the room together. Kirk walks past several covered bodies and then stops in front of the fourth one. He turns to face Clyde who seems slightly bewildered at the sight of so many corpses at one time. Kirk shakes his head as he pulls away the sheet covering Shirley Brewster. As Clyde's eyes fall upon her face he quickly turns away and seems very upset.

"How did she die?"

Kirk pulls the sheet over Shirley's face.

"I'm not sure."

Clyde seems confused.

"How can that be?"

Kyle glances at the other bodies.

"We'll know more when the CDC arrives tomorrow."

Clyde looks at Shirley's covered body again.

"But I thought you said?"

Kirk walks toward the door.

"There's been a rash of deaths in Castle Beach."

Clyde looks at Kirk oddly.

"Last night—I heard weird noises—like scratching."

From behind them they hear a sound.

"What was that?"

Page 123

Clyde and Kirk look each other. As they watch in horror several of the covered bodies begin to move. They react in shock for a few minutes. Clyde's face changes color as he watches in total disbelief as Shirley sits up on the metal table. As they stand there unable to move Shirley turns to face them and grins.

"This can't be real."

Clyde bolts for the door.

3
Night

The empty streets of Castle Beach appear to welcome the velvety softness of night as darkness approaches with glee. Oddly shaped shadows begin to dance as lawns suddenly take on a sinister feel where the feeling of oncoming danger seems to loom. A few sly cats skulk around as they begin their nightly hunt but otherwise a silent hush seems to blanket every front lawn.

4

David pulls Susan away from Preston's body as she begins to sob loudly. Her cries echo inside the marble-lined room.

"He can't be dead."

David glances at Kyle and Parker.

"There's nothing more we can do for him."

At that moment there is a scratching sound and they realize the coffin is opening. They seem frozen in place while time seems to stand still as a hand lifts the coffin lid upward.

5

"Thanks for the CDC info. I'll call you later."

Greg Petrie shuts off his cell phone and nervously glances at the front door. He leans back in his chair and sighs loudly.

"Why is the CDC coming to Castle Beach? They only show up when there's something really scary on the loose."

Page **124**

He stands up and walks to the door. He looks out and notices the silence blanketing the area. He turns around.

"Could it be? Is it possible?"

He glances at his cell phone on top of his desk.

6

Red drops line the hallway leading to the morgue and inside the entrance of the room. On the floor Kirk and Clyde lie within a few feet of each other with their eyes wide open but seeing nothing. No marks appear anywhere on their bodies.

7

Zabrina Relling is sitting on a bench in the backyard of her house looking completely dejected. She sighs as she looks back at the back door of her home. She wipes a tear from her eye.

"Oh Neil—I should've told you."

She seems about to cry.

"I should've told you."

She wipes another tear from her eye and as she turns around she sees a flash of color at the gate leading from the backyard. As she stares in shock she sees Neil Wainsright walking toward her with glowing yellow eyes. He holds his hand out to her. Without thinking she runs toward him and they embrace.

"Neil? Huh? How could you?"

Too late she realizes there is something different about Neil as she notices his bright yellow eyes rimmed with red luring her to let go of her fears. As she tries to pull away he grips her tightly and sinks his teeth into her neck in a vicious swipe. He laughs slyly and slurps joyfully as her life quickly fades away.

8

Jim Tyner stares in shock at the scene before him in the hallway. He shakes his head as he notices the bloody spots.

"What? Who could have done this?"

He slowly pushes the door open leading to the morgue and for a few seconds stare in horror at the scene in front of him not sure if it's real or not. His eyes fall on the empty metal tables where earlier had been bodies covered with white sheets.

9

Shadows dance throughout the crypt as David, Kyle, Susan, and Parker watch Thomas Nix come toward them. They back away as he grins broadly. His old-fashioned clothing glitters in the darkness, shooting off sparks of light with each step he takes. The velvet material of his jacket rustles loudly and echoes throughout the cavernous crypt as all four teenagers watch him with a mixture of morbid curiosity and fear. Kyle faces Parker.

"How can this thing?"

Parker glances at a stake lying on the floor nearby.

"Don't know."

David looks at Thomas with disgust.

"He killed Chris."

Parker seems to come alive upon hearing David's words and grabs the stake. Thomas reacts and begins laughing as he watches the small band of teenagers approaching him. Parker steps forward holding the stake in front of him. His eyes seem to be on fire as he looks at the stake and then at his undead foe.

"It's time you become mortal again."

Loud laughter erupts from deep within Thomas as he takes a step closer. Parker watches as Thomas focuses his stare on Susan. Her willpower disappears as David and Parker watch. She takes a step forward as Thomas edges closer. Not a sound can be heard inside the crypt as Susan's eyes lock with the undead being. He raises a hand slightly and without warning turns his attention on Parker. David watches as Parker drops the stake and stares helplessly at Thomas. Time freezes as both Parker and Susan appear to be caught in a spell of some sort.

"This frigging nightmare ends tonight."

David listens to his own words as he repeats them and glances at Kyle standing next to Parker. Thomas suddenly raises his hand and points to Susan and grins. His teeth sparkle in the darkness as she walks to him no longer seeming to be afraid. At that moment Parker seems to snap out of whatever control Thomas had over him. He looks at the stake on the floor beside him. He picks it up and turns to face David—attacking him in a violent rage. David is caught off guard as Parker attacks him and slams his fist into Parker's chest—knocking the air out of him. Parker falls on the floor and doubles over. David and Parker stare at each other as Kyle watches. Thomas then pulls Susan toward him as David suddenly grabs the stake from Parker's hand.

"What the fuck is wrong with you?"

Parker seems confused.

"I'm not sure—what—what just happened?"

At that moment they hear a scream as Thomas rips into Susan's neck. David turns to look at Susan in shock as she and Thomas appear to be floating above them as he feeds. They watch in horror unable to do anything. Parker stands up and reaches over to grab the bag of supplies. He pulls out a container of holy water and looks at it briefly. He looks over to where David and Kyle are standing—watching as Susan's screams fade away while loud sucking sounds echo throughout the crypt. Parker looks at the bottle of holy water in his hand once more and then without thinking he pulls the cover off and throws the bottle into the air at Thomas and Susan. As the water splashes onto Thomas he reacts to the scalding effect on his skin and falls to the floor with Susan. Blood gushes from her neck as David and Parker attack Thomas. Parker yells for Kyle to help them and as he and Kyle hold Thomas down—David begins pounding the stake into the chest of the man wearing old-fashioned clothing. Screams are heard as David relentlessly hammers away, unable to control his rage as he slams the hammer down on the wooden stake over and over. Blood sprays everywhere as each blow goes deeper.

Time stands still as anguished cries eventually become silent only to be replaced by sounds of heavy breathing as David continues to pound on the stake. He is still attacking the stake when he notices it slipping out of his hand. As he watches in stunned silence—the undead creature before him—which had lain in darkness for over two centuries waiting to be awakened—was finally at rest. The skin quickly turns to dust and then the clothing instantly falls away without a physical body to hold its shape.

"This is for Susan."

David turns to look at Parker and Kyle. They both seem unable to speak as all three of them watch in awe as the skeletal remains of Thomas Nix slowly turns into coarse white dust. Then it was over like it never happened. At that moment a cold gust of wind blows past them and out the door of the crypt. The room becomes silent again except for the sound of their breathing.

"Susan?"

David runs over to where Susan is lying—her throat badly mangled from the attack earlier. David slowly turns her over and looks at Parker and Kyle standing nearby realizing she's dead.

"Fuck him."

David strokes Susan's cheek.

"This wasn't supposed to end this way."

He begins to cry.

10

"We'll come back tomorrow for their bodies."

Parker closes the door to the mausoleum and pulls David toward the steps. They follow Kyle through the cemetery and into the woods. Darkness surrounds them as they pick their way through the trail in silence. Every now and then David turns to look back at the mausoleum until it fades from view. Chirpings of a few birds can be heard as they quietly walk through the woods. Suddenly sounds throughout the area are muted. They notice the eerie silence around them and stop several times to listen.

"Not a sound to be heard. You don't think?"

Suddenly the woods come alive as Chris attacks Kyle. As David and Parker fumble with the supply bag, looking for a stake

Page **128**

and hammer, Kyle screams for help as Chris drags him into the thick brush. David and Parker feel their way through the darkened area as they listen to Kyle's cries for help fade. There is a swishing sound and then they realize Chris is right behind them ready to attack. As he grabs Parker by the neck, David rams Chris with the stake in his hand. Chris cries out in pain as both Parker and David begin pounding the stake into his chest. Seconds seem to last forever as cries of pain echo through the woods only to be replaced by eerie silence shortly thereafter. David and Parker look at each other. The pain in their eyes is evident. They begin searching for Kyle and find him dead a few feet away.

"It isn't over yet."

Parker nods and looks toward the lights flickering in a distance. He looks back in the direction of the mausoleum.

"He waited for two hundred years."

David sighs loudly.

"He must have been attacked while he was in Boston and came home unaware he was dying. His family had no idea."

They begin walking along the path.

"They'll be waiting for us."

David wipes sweat from his brow.

"I know."

They reach the clearing and see Parker's car by the highway. There is not a shred of light anywhere as they slowly walk toward the car. Without a word between them David and Parker get into the car and drive back towards Castle Beach.

About the Series Creator

Gary Brin was born in 1965 and has lived in the United States Virgin Islands, Hawaii and California. He has edited numerous original literary works over the years—both new and revised. In 2019 he established Standish Press to bring forth interesting fictional and historical material usually ignored by mainstream publishers because of specific views or content. In addition to publishing books, he also created the Nancy Hanks Lincoln Public Library (named after the mother of Abraham Lincoln) in 2014 to make available hard-to-find books to a worldwide audience.

Production Notes

Written by Wesley Adams and Daphne McGee
Manuscript edited by Gary Brin
Cover photograph from Wikimedia Commons
Front cover design and interior book layout by Gary Brin
Cover layout by Victoria Valentine
Additional help provided by Carlton J. Young
Series created by Gary Brin

Character List

Colin Barclay
Rodney Bellingham
Megan Bowers
Matt Brewster
Shirley Brewster
Claire Cassell
Clarissa Cassell
Natalie Cassell
Milton Donovan
Wendy Emerson
George Fisher
Barry Fowler
Cole Franklin
Chris Gibson
Emma Jahnston
Luke Jennings
Malcolm Kingsbury
Susan Lancaster
Andrew Latimer
Ingrid Mifflin
Lisa Morgan
Thomas Nix
Ivy Patterson
Maxwell Pendergraft
Carson Penney
Chandler Penney
Simon Penney
Greg Petrie
Ethan Polzoni
Mark Relling
Zabrina Relling
Zachary Relling

Abigail Ross
Justine Ross
Parker Ross
Jessica Sago
Juliet Sago
Preston Sago
Melora Schubb
Daphne Shaw
David Sherwood
Isabel Stamos
Marlisa Turner
Jim Tyner
Neil Wainsright
Clyde Walker
Kyle Webster
John Weddleton
Kirk Wheeling
Jeremy Winterfield

Real People Mentioned

Sarah Michelle Gellar
Stephen King

Next in the Series
Book 5
Ocean Landing

www.ingramcontent.com/pod-product-compliance
Lightning Source LLC
Chambersburg PA
CBHW060803210726
48292CB00013B/1745